Last Stand

By
Duane Boehm

Last Stand

Copyright 2014 Duane Boehm

For more information or permission contact:
boehmduane@gmail.com

This book is a work of fiction. References to real people, events, establishments, organizations, or locales are intended only to provide a sense of authenticity and are used fictitiously. All other characters, and all incidents and dialogue are drawn from the author's imagination and not to be construed as real.

ISBN: 1-500-67256-4

Other Books by Duane Boehm

In Just One Moment
Last Chance: A Gideon Johann Western Book 2
Last Hope: A Gideon Johann Western Book 3
Last Ride: A Gideon Johann Western Book 4
Last Breath: A Gideon Johann Western Book 5
Last Journey: A Gideon Johann Western Book 6
Last Atonement: A Gideon Johann Western Book 7
*Wanted: A Collection of Western Stories (7
authors)*

Dedicated to my father, John Melvin Boehm and all the rest of us that are cowboys at heart

Chapter 1

The day was beautiful, one of those spring afternoons that a boy had to get out in and celebrate the end of winter. Earlier in the morning, eight-year-old Benjamin Oakes had suffered through his pa's Sunday morning sermon and now was exploring for gold by walking a creek that ran through their small Colorado ranch. He loved this time of year. The mountains were still covered in snow for the most part and he had a good view of the big one to the north that he called Old Man. When he stared at it until his eyes got glazy, he could imagine the face of an old wrinkled man. Everything below the mountains was turning green with the grass coming to life and the trees starting to leaf out. Even the air seemed fresher from the spring rains and new growth.

He had wandered far enough from home in his quest for riches that he kept looking over his shoulder for his momma. There was enough rock and brush to give him some cover, but that woman could track like an Indian when it came to finding him. His last expedition was still fresh in his mind with the memory of her hunting him down and tanning him all the way back to the cabin. With his attention divided between looking for anything shining in the creek bed and fears of being caught, he about jumped out of his skin when a horse nickered at him. Diving behind a bush, he feared the worst. His pa had always said that this was a country that discretion was the better part of valor. Off the main paths, there were way more ruffians and occasional Indian parties than there were well-wishers. Peeking through the branches, he saw the saddled horse looking his way and a man on the ground next to it. There was enough red on his clothes to know that he was not there sleeping. His first instinct was to run home, but he had never seen a dead man before and he was curious. Visions of claiming the guns and horse also held him in place. He decided to stay put for a good while checking things out and working up his courage to walk up to them. Once he finally stood, the horse nickered again and bobbed its head, drawing him slowly to it and the man. He had goose bumps so bad that it made him shiver and his legs trembled.

"Christ Almighty, what a sight," the boy said as he reached the horse and man.

The cowboy looked as if he had been used for target practice with bullet holes and blood everywhere. His pistol and rifle were beside him as well as several spent cartridges. A streak of blood was painted down a large rock that he had apparently leaned against before succumbing to his injuries and sliding to the ground. Only his hat appeared to come through the ordeal unscathed, sitting on the ground as if placed there by a beau on a picnic.

Benjamin wondered if getting shot hurt a lot. He prided himself in being tough when his momma pulled a splinter out of him, but this sure appeared as if it was painful from the looks of the man. The size of the holes in the man's clothes and all the blood sure made it look as if bullets hurt.

One time he had snuck his pa's forbidden hunting knife out of the cabin so he could get a good look at it. He took it around back and was admiring it and feeling its sharp edge. Until he saw blood, he had no idea that he had cut his finger. He hoped for this man's sake that it had been like that, but he had his doubts.

The man seemed to be plenty dead, but Benjamin gave his boot a good kick just to make sure. The cowboy let out a loud groan that startled Benjamin so badly that the hair on his neck stood up and he had to squeeze hard to keep from pissing all over himself.

The man opened his eyes long enough to see the boy. During the night, he had come to the realization that no one would find him out here and even if they did, he was probably too far gone. Luck was only reason that he had made it to his thirty-seventh birthday anyway. He made his peace with dying, accepting that this was the way it would end. Live by the sword; die by the sword. He had then prayed for forgiveness for an accidental act that he had committed years ago and that still haunted him every day of his life. He did not believe that it was a forgivable sin, but he felt serene afterward and dozed off not expecting to wake again. When the kid kicked his boot and jarred his whole body, he thought he was waking up in Hell. If he had more strength, he would have laughed aloud at the irony of being found by a young boy.

Benjamin had always been taught by his momma and pa that he should help those in need and in his eight years of life, he had never seen someone so in need. He could ride pretty well, but getting in the saddle was the problem. After several failed attempts, he led the horse beside some large rocks. Climbing them, he was able to mount. He said "Giddy-up" and put his heels into the horse a little bit and it took off as if somebody had put a match under its ass. Its ears were pinned back and the animal was in a full gallop. They were going faster than he had ever ridden in his life and he was holding onto the saddle horn for dear life while gripping with his legs Indian style since he could not reach the stirrups. The buckskin was bridle broke and followed his direction home, jumping ditches and rocks as if it knew it was on a life and death mission.

Benjamin's pa, Ethan, stepped out of the cabin with his rifle, planning to ride out and check on the herd. He caught sight of the fast charging rider and set his rifle handily against the porch rail. The horseman appeared to be small or was leaning forward to make himself appear so and he was certainly in a hurry to get to the cabin. Ethan's eyes grew large with surprise when the rider was close enough to see that it was his son.

Stress was stamped all over the boy's face when he reined the horse up in the yard. Ethan, hoping not to add to the tension, tried to sound as casual as if it were a normal conversation, "Looks like you have run into some trouble. What happened, son?" he asked.

Benjamin started spewing words so fast that his father had to concentrate to understand him. "Pa, I was out exploring and I found this man shot all to pieces with blood all over and I kicked his boot cause I thought he was dead and he groaned and so I took his horse to go get you," he said all in one breath.

"Where is he?" Ethan asked calmly.

"He is near that rock that you call Lot," Benjamin said.

"You did good, Benjamin," Ethan said as he lifted his son out of the saddle.

"There is blood everywhere and the poor man is a mess," Benjamin said.

"How big of a man is he?" Ethan asked.

The boy thought for a moment and said, "I'm pretty sure that he is not near as tall as you and he is thin."

"We should be able to get him in the wagon ourselves then," his father remarked.

"What is going on?" Ethan's wife, Sarah, asked as she stepped out onto the porch.

With emphasis on his first two words, Ethan said, "Your son has been out exploring and found a man that has been shot. I am going to go hitch up the wagon and see if we can get to him. You probably need to come along to help lift him and do some doctoring."

"I'll get some blankets and whatever else we have. It is the least that I can do since the son that I apparently conceived by myself found him," Sarah said as she whisked back through the door of the cabin.

Ethan loved Sarah's feistiness. It meant that sometimes he was on the losing end of an argument, but the woman kept things lively. He had met her at a Colorado Stock Growers Association social when he was in Denver for one of their meetings. The combination of beauty and sassiness had smitten him from the start and in the ensuing long-distance courting, it seemed to him that only his tenacity and not much else had been the deciding factor in winning her hand over all the other suitors. After he brought her back as his wife, many of the women around did not care for her brashness, but nobody ever walked all over her.

Sarah had noticed Ethan that first night well before he made his fumbling attempt at conversation. He towered over most men and had the muscle to go with it. With his blond hair and broad shoulders, he made quite a dashing figure. She had even found his awkwardness charming, though she was never one to show her hand. Over the next year, she had strung him along making him think he was in competition with other men for her heart when in actuality the others would have had to sweep her off her feet to have had a chance. There was a goodness and humor to Ethan that reminded her a little of her father and the only reason she had drawn out the courtship was to make sure that Ethan had enough determination in him to fight for what he wanted. Once he proved to be up to the challenge, the coyness stopped and the real romancing started.

"Do you think we can save him, Pa?" Benjamin asked as they walked to the barn.

"I don't know. He sounds bad, but we will try our best," Ethan said.

"I didn't mean to hurt him, honest. I was just checking to see if he was dead," Benjamin said as he looked up at his father.

Ethan rubbed his son's head and said, "That might have saved his life. You would not have rushed back on his horse if you thought he was dead and he now knows he has a reason to keep living."

"Is Momma mad?' Benjamin continued.

"No, I just fired her up a little to help keep her mind off worrying so much about this. You and I both know that when she is mad, you don't have to ask to figure it out," Ethan said and winked at his son.

The trip to retrieve the man involved crossing the creek three times to find a suitable path for the wagon and even with that they had to hold on for all that they were worth to keep from being thrown about the buckboard. Once they reached the spot, Sarah took one look and then covered her mouth with her hand, closed her eyes, and shook her head. There was just no way that she could prepare herself for this. Ethan climbed off the wagon and helped his wife down before looking over the carnage.

"The guy is a fighter. I will give him that and he certainly is welled armed. That pistol is one of those Colt Frontiers that I have been telling you about and that is the prettiest Winchester 73 that I have ever seen. Looks like he held his attacker off long enough that they had had enough," he said with a touch of begrudging admiration.

Sarah was checking the man over and said, "Those guns did not keep him from getting shot all up, but he is still breathing. We best get him back and not dally."

The man was medium height and thin. Ethan grabbed him under the arms and Benjamin and Sarah each took a leg. He groaned loudly when they lifted him, but did not open his eyes or offer any resistance as they maneuvered him into the wagon. Sarah and Benjamin rode in the back with him, trying to hold him in place through the rough ride back to the cabin. They managed to get him to their home and into Benjamin's bed still alive. He had not opened his eyes the whole time, only moaning occasionally when they hit a bump.

"I've never seen so much blood in my whole life and the ride got it going again," Sarah said.

"Me either, but we had to get him back here. There was no other choice," Ethan said.

"He's going to die isn't he?" Sarah asked as she wiped the sweat from the man's face with a rag.

Ethan did not answer, but instead said, "Since his horse is already saddled, I'm going to take it to town to get Doc."

"I'll try and get some water down him," Sarah said.

"Go ahead and strip him down. You'll have to cut that shirt off him and maybe his trousers too to start cleaning him. I'm sure you won't see anything that you haven't seen before," Ethan said and winked at her, trying to get her to smile and relax a little.

"Ethan Oakes, some of the things that you say, and then to preach on Sunday. And besides, you forgot that I have my son that you were not taking ownership of today so maybe I will see something new," she shot back.

Ethan gave her a kiss and said, "That was the old rancher in me talking, not the new preacher, and he loves it when you talk like that. I'll get back as quickly as I can."

He put the buckskin into an easy lope and headed towards town. The ride gave him time to think about the situation. Ethan had been born here and over the years he had encountered just about every kind of man that chose to hang their hat in Colorado. It did not seem likely to him that the man had been hunted down. Whoever shot him would not have likely been satisfied to leave him alive and returning fire at them, especially if he had a bounty on his head. The cowboy could have accidently surprised someone not wanting to be discovered and paid the price, but if he had to guess, he suspected the man had been after the people that shot him and was ambushed. Either way, he hoped he would not come to regret putting the man under his roof.

Less than three hours later, he was riding back into his yard. The trip home seemed as if it had taken forever as his mind wandered over all the possible scenarios the cowboy might bring upon his family. He let the horse have its fill of water and then put it in the barn.

Entering Benjamin's room, he found his son standing attentively at the foot of the bed and his wife sitting beside the man, trying to get him to drink water. Both Sarah and Benjamin had concern etched on their faces and he noticed that the room now had a pungent smell of sweat and sickness.

"Doc Abram is on his way. He took off before I did and I passed him on the way back. He is coming as fast as that horse and buggy will allow," Ethan said.

"I've gotten some water down him and cleaned him up. It looks like he is shot in the thigh, side, and up in the shoulder area. All on the left side. I don't think he is really conscious. He hasn't opened his eyes once," Sarah said.

"Is he still bleeding?" Ethan asked.

"I got it slowed way down. I think the wagon ride about did him in," she said.

"I went through his saddlebags in town while I let the horse cool down and he travels light. There wasn't any identification that I could find. Just a half of a bottle of whiskey, some food, change of clothes, and some money," he told her.

"Do you think he is an outlaw?" Sarah asked.

"I don't know, but the man knows horseflesh. That buckskin loped all the way to town and could have gone farther," Ethan told her.

An hour later, Doctor Abram came trotting up in his buggy. The doctor was up in his sixties, having spent his entire career in the town of Last Stand. He had delivered both Ethan and Benjamin and had treated pretty much every injury or sickness known to man in the little town.

The doctor was known for his congeniality as long as no one got his dander up. After the war, the area was overran with ruffians and one named Durango Dick showed up at his door wounded and brandishing his pistol. "Doc, I need you to fix me up," he said when the doctor opened his door.

"Put your gun away and I will see what I can do for you," the doctor said.

"Maybe you don't understand, but I got the gun and I make the rules," Dick said as he waved the gun about in his agitated state.

"Now put your gun up and I can help you. A gun is not necessary," the doctor said in a measured tone.

"Damn it, I ain't telling you again," Dick roared at him while still waving his pistol at the doctor.

The doctor calmly reached for his shotgun behind the door and blasted Durango Dick into the street before the outlaw even realized what was happening.

Walking out into the street and standing over the dead man he said, "You were right. I just treated you with your gun drawn."

After word spread of the incident, the doctor found he had gained a completely new respect from the rougher side of society. No one ever showed up at his place with a gun drawn again.

Ethan greeted the doctor at the door and led the elder man to the bedroom. Doctor Abram pulled the sheet back on the man and gave him a quick look. "That man has lost a lot of blood. He has no color," he said.

"I think it happened yesterday. It looked like he had been there for a while and some of the blood was already dry," Ethan said.

"Sarah, would you please get me some hot water? I will need to clean him up again after I get done examining his wounds," the doctor said.

Sarah went to heat the water and then started supper while Ethan and Benjamin played checkers at the table. Neither was really concentrating on their game, but it beat sitting and waiting. An occasional groan escaped the bedroom, causing the family to all exchange glances. As Sarah finished preparing the meal, the doctor shuffled out of the bedroom.

"If there is anything lucky about getting shot all to hell, that cowboy is lucky that the bullets missed his organs and bones and exited clean. He has lost so much blood that I still do not expect him to live and he could get an infection from going so long without treatment. I dosed the wounds with iodine and I'll show you what to do" the doctor said.

"We put an extra plate out for you, Doc. Join us for supper and then you can show Sarah," Ethan said.

"I may be old, but I know good food when I smell it," Doc Abram said as he sat down at the table.

"I'm much obliged that you came out here, Doc," Ethan said.

"You're good people, but I don't know why you didn't just leave him where you found him and go get the sheriff. Maybe the scoundrel would have died by then and the world would be rid of one more heathen," the doctor said.

"Doc Abram, how could you say that? All of us have a duty to help those in need. Especially you a doctor," Sarah admonished.

"Sarah, I have never turned down a patient, unless you count Durango Dick, I guess. I am just saying that I think you should have handled it differently and not brought who knows what into your home. Over the years, I have patched up plenty like him only to do it again or watch them die," he said.

Ethan interjected, "Doc, we do not know a thing about this man. I refuse to suppose the worst until I know differently. He could be a victim like any of us could be."

"I suppose, but I doubt it. I just don't want you folks to be endangered for your good nature," the doctor said before changing the subject to cattle.

After the meal and showing Sarah how to treat the wounds, the doctor said his goodbyes and then paused at the door. "Ethan, do you want me to send the sheriff out in the morning to see if he has a poster on your cowboy? You might have some reward money due," he said.

"No, we'll see if he lives before we worry about that. I'll pray that he does and it is for a higher purpose than going to jail or the gallows," Ethan said.

Chapter 2

The next morning, Ethan awoke before dawn. He had tossed and turned all night, never going into a deep sleep, while managing only to fall into a slumber with wild dreams about the man dying and haunting the cabin. Preacher or not, he did not cherish the thought of waking up with a dead man in his home. He lit a lamp and then dawdled about before finally entering Benjamin's bedroom. The man was motionless except for the slight movement of his chest with each breath. There did not appear to be any change in his appearance, but his breathing seemed less labored.

Ethan went to make some coffee and almost tripped over Benjamin asleep on the pallet that they had made for him in the main room of the cabin. After the coffee was ready, he sat at the table, drinking it and watching the sky begin to lighten. Early morning was his favorite time of the day, allowing him to plan his activities before the family was up and demanding his attention. After it was light enough to see, he went out and busied himself with the chores.

By the time he returned, Sarah was cooking breakfast. The aroma of bacon, eggs, and biscuits filled the room and made his mouth water to the accompaniment of his growling belly. His wife knew how to cook a fine meal. Sitting down at the table, he watched her flutter about and asked, "Have you checked on him?"

"No, I was afraid he might be dead and I did not want to see that alone," Sarah said.

"He was alive when I went to do the chores. I think maybe he was breathing easier," Ethan said.

"After breakfast, we can see if he is conscious and treat his wounds," she said.

Sarah continued her bee like breakfast preparation until she turned and caught Ethan staring at her backside. "You can forget about that this morning. Rouse Benjamin up, please," she said.

Ethan smiled and got up to wake Benjamin, who was still exhausted from the big day he had experienced yesterday. Normally, Benjamin was an easy riser, but Ethan had to shake his son a couple of times and get him talking before he was satisfied he was awake.

Breakfast lacked its usual jovial mood. Except for Benjamin's inquiry about the cowboy, there was little conversation and they unconsciously rushed their eating to the point that none of them enjoyed the food. Benjamin did not even bother to make his normal production out of bursting his egg yolks before sopping them up with a biscuit. The cowboy was weighing heavily on all their minds.

After they finished the meal, Benjamin was sent to feed the chickens while Ethan and Sarah took a fresh pitcher of water and a biscuit with them to the room. Sunlight from the window bathed the cowboy, almost giving him the appearance of a peaceful resting guest and making a stark contrast to the condition that they had found him in the previous day.

"His color is better. He actually looks more alive than dead this morning," Sarah commented.

At the sound of her voice, the man opened his eyes in a vacant stare, revealing a piercing blue color. Ethan, standing at the foot of the bed, reacted by pulling his head and shoulders back as if he were trying to avoid walking into a spider web. The hair on his arms and neck stood up and the goose bumps gave him a chill. For some reason the stranger's face had given him a jolt of nostalgia. This was the first time that he had really bothered to notice his features.

"What is it?" Sarah asked.

"I don't know. When he opened his eyes it was like I almost recognized him," Ethan said.

"Surely you would know if you knew him," she said.

"You would think, but those blue eyes and that unruly hair and that Greek nose. Like maybe I knew him a long -," Ethan stopped midsentence. Grabbing the sheet, he uncovered the man's left leg and turned it to see his calf. It had a badly scarred indentation across it from an injury that had occurred years ago.

"Oh, my God. It's Gideon. When he was a teenager, a Longhorn turned on him, goring his leg, and killing the horse that he was riding. He limped for a year," Ethan said before pausing to do a calculation in his head. "I guess it has been eighteen years since I last laid eyes upon him. I sure never thought that this day would happen."

Sarah had been hearing stories about Gideon Johann since Ethan and she had been dating. The two had grown up best friends on neighboring ranches. Gideon had been the free-spirit leader in their mischievous escapades of youth. Ethan had told tales that had left her picturing a light-hearted and funny boy that was hard to reconcile with the unfortunate man lying in the bed. His mother had died when he was seventeen and the next year, in 1861, he and his father had joined the Second Colorado Infantry. Ethan had received letters regularly about his life as a soldier. Gideon had been particularly excited when the infantry had consolidated into the Second Colorado Cavalry. After that, he wrote a grieving letter about his father's death at the Battle of Little Blue River. Ethan had received one more letter after that and then never heard from him again. After so much time, the letters were still sitting neatly tied in the bottom of the blanket chest. Over the years, rumors of his whereabouts would come in, but nobody from the area had ever actually seen or heard from him.

Ethan had to sit down to take it all in. His body had gone limp on him. He kept staring at the face to keep convincing himself that it really was Gideon. "I just can't fathom how after all this time, he ends up here like this. I wonder what brought him back and why he was shot," he remarked.

"Do you think he is an outlaw?" Sarah asked.

"I don't think so. All the rumors had him being a deputy, ranch hand, or gunman. I think we would have heard about it if he were wanted," Ethan said.

The bandages had only spots of blood on them when Sarah removed them. She checked the tissue and then poured the iodine into the wounds. There was no pus and the wounds did not look infected to her. They were able to get some water down him, but he never opened his eyes again.

"I think I will try to get some milk down him later. He is going to have to have some nourishment before long," Sarah said.

Lost in thought, Ethan said, "I just can't believe it. What are the odds our son finds a man barely alive that happens to be the best friend I ever had that has been missing for eighteen years?"

"I'd say about the same as you deciding to start preaching a couple of years ago," Sarah said.

Ethan looked up blankly at her, missing her attempt at humor or any other messages that may have been buried in the statement. She smiled at him to try to get him to come out of his stupor.

He thought for a moment more and then smiled back. "Yeah, you are right about that. I guess they are both mighty long odds. Maybe there is higher reason for all of this," he said.

Ethan had never been an overly religious man, but the family attended church every Sunday and he always listened to the sermon. Over time, he began to read the Bible in the evenings. One night he was reading the Gospel of Mark when passages 12:30 and 12:31, "And thou shalt love the Lord thy God with all thy heart, and with all thy soul, and with all thy mind, and with all thy strength: this *is* the first commandment" and "Thou shalt love thy neighbor as thyself. There is none other commandment greater than these", spoke to him like nothing he had ever before read. He kept rereading the passages, deciding to become a student of the Bible.

Eventually, their preacher moved away and the congregation asked Ethan to take his place. It had been shaky going at first, but over time, he had developed into an engaging speaker. His sermons were a far cry from the Hell and Brimstone deliveries of his predecessor, causing some to leave, but the church grew with his gentler message of love and goodness.

Sometimes, he was conflicted over his Sunday sermons and the fact that out on the ranch, he always took precautions when a stranger showed up, fearful that they might be out to do them harm. He could never come up with a resolution, knowing that carelessness would get a man killed.

"Sarah, I am going to ride out and check the cattle. I need some time to think and I planned to do it yesterday before all the excitement anyway," Ethan said.

"Take your time. I have things under control here, but before you go, light a fire under Benjamin or he is going to be late for school," Sarah told him.

He walked out to the barn and saddled his favorite horse that he called Pie, a piebald gelding that he had traded for in town. It had once been an Indian pony and was larger than most. He had almost given up on ever getting it to accept a saddle, but with patience, he finally won over the horse. The animal was the surest footed he had ever owned and had the stamina to be ridden all day.

He put Pie into a lope and headed for Pint Ridge. On the other side of the crest was Sweet Valley. In the spring months, the basin was the first place on his ranch to green up and the cattle always stayed there until they ate it down and moved on to a new spot.

The air was cool, but with the clear sky, the sun was already taking the edge off the chill. As he got into the rhythm of the horse's movement, he started to relax and feel like himself again even if he still could not imagine anything that could have been more shocking than the turn of events that morning. He needed this ride to think and come to terms with things. His mind was still having trouble grasping that a man that years ago, he had given up on ever seeing again was lying in his house barely alive. In some ways, he wished it did not matter to him anymore, but the feeling of getting punched in the gut once he realized that the man was Gideon told him otherwise.

Both of them had been the brother that the other never had. Gideon was an only child and he had four sisters to drive him crazy. They had become friends when they were seven years old starting out in school. Over the course of their youth, they had been constant companions, always hunting, fishing, and helping out on both ranches.

Ethan had been there the day the bull gored Gideon's horse and his leg in the process. Gideon and he had been driving the herd to the other side of the ranch where the grass was better. They were going at a leisurely pace, riding close enough together to be able to carry on a conversation. The young bull was in front of Gideon when it planted its front legs and kicked its rear around before charging. It happened so quickly that there was not even time to shout. Ethan could still remember the pain and shock on Gideon's face when it gored them. The bull stood there with its horn stuck in the horse's side as the animal slowly sunk to the ground while Gideon managed to slide off before it pinned him. He was barely able to stand and helpless as the bull stomped its foot and freed its horn. Ethan had spurred his horse, locked arms with Gideon, and swung him on behind while on a dead run before the bull had time to attack. He thought Gideon was going to bleed to death that time too. His horse almost gave out carrying the two riders into town in a run. Gideon was badly hurt, but Dr. Abram managed to save his leg.

They never talked about that day. Gideon had said, "Thank you. You saved my life, partner." After that, the subject never came up again.

After Gideon started courting Abigail Schone a couple of years before he joined the war, Ethan found himself the odd man out a lot of the time. They still managed to hunt and fish together, but it was obvious that Gideon was head over hills in love. After Gideon volunteered for the infantry, Ethan tried to talk his father into letting him join also, but he would not hear of it, and being a loner, he continued to fish and hunt by himself, but the fun was all gone from it. Most of his time was spent looking at one end of a cow or the other. The letters helped some, though the things described in them left him anxious for Gideon's safety. After the notes abruptly stopped, he actually mourned, fearing that Gideon had died. In time, he came to accept it as the death of a friendship.

Now there were so many questions to be answered. Was he in trouble with the law? Why did he come back now after all this time? Where had he been all these years? On and on and on, but most of all – what happened and why did he not stay in touch?

He reached the top of Pint Ridge and pulled Pie up to look into the valley. Below him, he could see his herd scattered about grazing on the new grass with several newborn calves nursing on their mommas. Spring was his favorite time of the year. The ranch renewed itself all green again and there were all the new calves to check.

He put the horse into a walk headed towards the herd. The calves made him think about the spring that Benjamin was born when he and Sarah got into a big fight over what to name him. He had wanted to name him Gideon. Sarah had been adamant that it was silly to name a child after someone that did not care enough about him to stay in touch all those years. Her words had stung, but he knew that she was right. They eventually decided to name him after his father who had died the previous year.

Riding through the herd, he counted seven new calves. They were the first this spring and all had been born since he had checked the herd three days ago. The births were a good start to the season and he did not see any cows that looked as if they had lost their calf.

Once he was clear of the herd, he put Pie into a run and headed for home. The horse needed the exercise and he wanted to just focus on riding and not think anymore. He had to hold his hat down to keep it from flying off as they charged up the ridge. Sometimes from lack of necessity, he forgot how much Pie loved to run. It seemed as if they might take off in flight when they hit the peak and he let out a whoop of joy as they headed down the other side. Nothing had been resolved with his ride, but he felt better and ready to meet whatever was ahead.

Ethan was surprised to see Doc Abram's buggy in front of the cabin. He did not expect the doctor to check on the patient again so soon considering his low opinion of the situation.

Doc was listening to Gideon's chest with a stethoscope and Sarah was in the corner cutting up some new bandages when Ethan entered the room. He noticed that neither of their faces showed the strain of yesterday in treating their patient.

"I got some milk down him while you were gone. He still has not opened his eyes again though," Sarah said when she saw Ethan come in.

"Good. Glad to hear it," Ethan said.

"Your cowboy here is better. His heart is stronger and he has more color, but he needs to wake up so he can start eating," Doc said.

"Do you think he has a head injury?" Sarah asked.

"No, I think that it is shock and the loss of blood. The milk will help some. Give him as much as you can," the doctor told her.

"Did you tell Doc?" Ethan asked Sarah.

"No, I thought I would let you," she said.

Doc looked up at Ethan. "Tell me what?"

"Look at his left calf, Doc," Ethan said.

The doctor moved the sheet to look and then did a quick glance at the face. "Well, I'll be damn. That's Gideon Johann," he said.

"I could hardly believe it," Ethan said.

"I guess you did do the right thing by retrieving him. Gideon was a good boy. I always liked him," Doc said as he rubbed his chin in surprise. "I cannot believe it. How long has he been gone, Ethan?"

"Eighteen years now," Ethan answered.

"I always wondered what happened to that boy. That kid had some grit. I guess we know now why he is still alive. I thought sure that leg would get gangrene from all that cow shit and I'd have to saw it off, but he proved me wrong and I expect he will this time too," Doc said.

"I appreciate you coming out here and tending to him, Doc," Ethan said.

The old doctor smiled at Ethan and said, "This should really get the tongues a wagging in Last Stand."

∞

Later in the afternoon, Sarah was out in the yard cussing under her breath as she tried to corner a chicken for dinner when she saw Benjamin running up the road. Her son never hurried back from school and her first thought was that he must have encountered the men that shot Gideon. She started to run to meet him, but was already worn out from chicken chasing and stopped to wait for him.

"What is it, Benjamin?" Sarah asked in a worried tone.

"I was hurrying home so I could take my turn watching over the man I found," Benjamin said.

Sarah started building into a fury to unleash on her son for scaring her for no reason, but checked her emotion at seeing Benjamin standing there beaming with pride and wanting to help. She put her arm around his shoulder and started walking to the cabin. "That would be a big help to me. Do you remember hearing your pa talk about his friend Gideon that disappeared after the war? Well you found your pa's best friend and saved his life," she told him.

"Really? I bet Pa is real happy," Benjamin said.

"I think he is, but he is kind of surprised by it all right now. I wouldn't pester him with a lot of questions just yet," Sarah said.

After they reached the bedroom, Benjamin said, "I am going to be quiet and do my schoolwork and if something happens, I will come get you."

Pride welled up in Sarah. Her little man was growing up and becoming a lot like his father. She bent over and kissed him on top of the head. "Thank you. I really appreciate it," she said and left the room.

Benjamin stared at Gideon, watching the slight movement of the cover as he breathed. He had heard so many stories about the man that he had expected him to be near giant in size. He certainly was not what Benjamin had imagined.

"Mr. Gideon, my name is Benjamin Oakes and my pa is Ethan. I found you and I am going to help you get well. I think Pa is going to be real happy when you get better and start talking. When he told me stories about you, I could tell that he missed you."

Chapter 3

Doctor Abram was universally considered the leading gossip in Last Stand. Between his practice and his habit of stopping by the Last Stand Last Chance Saloon, there was very little that happened in the area that he did not know about or repeat. He liked to sit at a table in the saloon, drinking beer and holding court. By noon the day after his second visit to Ethan's place, the town was abuzz with news of the return of Gideon Johann. The doctor gave out his original diagnosis of the likely death of Gideon, figuring that if he took a turn for the worse, that people would already be prepared for it, and if he lived, it would make the story all the better.

Gideon's absence had taken on a life of its own over the years. The few bits of information that reached Last Stand had only added to the mystery until everybody had their own theory concerning his whereabouts, what he had been involved in, and why he never returned. He had become a kind of mythical figure by simply disappearing.

∞

Ethan and Sarah walked out onto the porch after eating lunch to enjoy the warm sunny day. She was going to sit with him as he smoked a pipe and then go tend to Gideon while Ethan checked the shoes on the horses. Sarah saw the rider first and immediately recognized who it was from the skirt hanging over each side of the saddle.

"Looks like Abigail Hanson is paying us a visit. I wish I could learn to straddle a horse with a skirt on like she does," Sarah said in admiration.

"I wonder what brings her out this way?" Ethan asked.

Sarah looked at him as if he was as dense as a log. Before finally settling for Marcus Hanson as a husband, the former Abigail Schone had waited years for the return of Gideon. She had been considered the most eligible girl around before most of the bachelors gave up on courting her, convinced that she would become a spinster waiting for Gideon's return. Marcus, with patience and persistence, had finally won her over after years of rejection.

"Well, if I had to guess, I would say that our gossipy doctor has got word out all over the county that Gideon is here and she has come to have a look for herself," she said as if her deduction was the most obvious fact in the world.

"You really think so?" Ethan asked.

Sarah, annoyed that her husband could be so clueless, shook her head and said, "Ethan, sometimes you are as naïve as a child. How many times over the years has Abby just showed up out of the blue at our door for a visit?"

Before he could answer, Abigail was within hearing distance so he let the question hang.

"Ethan, Sarah, I guess you know why I am here. I am not going to pretend that this is just a social visit. I was in town and Doc Abram made a point of coming up to me and telling me about Gideon. That man takes a real delight in gossiping. He told me how badly Gideon was shot up and I figured since I wasted all those years of my life waiting for him to return that I was entitled to a peek at him before he died, if you don't mind," Abigail said in her no nonsense tone.

When Sarah had first moved to Last Stand after marrying Ethan, she and Abigail had not taken to each other. Being two of the prettier women in the area, and both independent and opinionated, they each viewed the other as an adversary. Over time, they had come to find that they had much more in common with each other than with most of the women in the area. They began to seek each other out when they needed to have an intelligent conversation with another woman and commiserate over the solitude of ranch life until they had become close friends.

"If anybody has the right to see him, it is you. He is not conscious, but you can have a look at him," Sarah said before pausing and smiling. "You're not planning on finishing him off are you?"

The awkwardness was broken and Abigail smiled mischievously. "No, I will wait to see if he recovers before I kill him," she said.

Ethan and Sarah stayed on the porch when Abigail went inside the cabin. She paused at the doorway to the bedroom and took a deep breath. Her heart was pounding in her chest as if it were a blacksmith's hammer and she felt so flush that she wondered if she was having her first hot flash. She willed herself into the room and looked down at him. His face was not as aged as she had been expecting. In fact, she thought he looked much the same as in his youth. He was more gaunt and the sun and wind had taken away some of the softness from his skin, but the man was definitely Gideon. There was a scar that had not been there. It started on his left cheekbone and went straight down about an inch, but overall it looked as if the last eighteen years had not been overly cruel to him.

She cursed herself under her breath for what she was feeling. She was a wife and a mother and it was wrong to feel like a giddy schoolgirl about a man that had disappeared a lifetime ago, but there was no denying what everyone always said about your first love. The emotion welled up in her like spring water pushing through the soil.

Abigail quickly flicked a tear away and then checked the door to make sure that no one was watching. She picked up his left hand with the two of hers and then gave him a kiss on the forehead. Sitting down in the chair, she held his hand, reminiscing about their days of courting. Mainly, she remembered the laughter. Gideon had been so funny and lighthearted, going to great lengths to make her giggle. The recollections made her realize how little humor was in her life these days.

"I sure never thought that I would catch sight of you again in this lifetime and I doubt that I would have if somebody had not shot you. It has been a long, long time," Abby said.

Abby studied Gideon's face and rubbed his hand. She had to convince herself that after all these years she was really looking at him. "Damn you, Gideon Johann. You wasted your life and made me settle for a second place marriage. Winnie could have been your daughter and we could have had a whole passel more," she told him.

She checked the doorway again and leaned in and whispered, "There are things you should have known about if you hadn't done your damn disappearing act," She then fluttered out of the room so mad that she actually had thoughts of murder on her mind. Stopping at the front door, she collected herself before joining Ethan and Sarah on the porch.

"Thank you for allowing me to see him. I know coming here was silly, but I just had to see him alive one more time. He really has not changed that much. I was surprised," Abigail said.

"I did not recognize him until he opened his eyes. Of course, I was not thinking about it being him and you

LAST STAND • 27

knew it was Gideon. I guess that makes the difference," Ethan said to make conversation.

Sarah noticed that Abigail assumed Gideon was on his deathbed. "Abby, Doc told us that he thinks he has a chance to live," she said.

Abigail's face lost all expression with only her eyelids blinking rapidly as if given a sharp slap by surprise. Thinking that he was dying and then learning that he had a fighting chance was such juxtaposition that it made her swoony. To end the lull in the conversation, she said, "Really? That old saw-bones is telling everybody in town that he is not going to make it. It's a good thing he is a fine doctor or somebody would shoot him one of these days for his stories."

Ethan and Sarah exchanged glances that served as a whole conversation about what they had just seen.

"Abby, I am doing everything that I can for him. He has improved, just never really woke up," Sarah said.

"Oh, I know you are. This was just a silly schoolgirl idea of mine to come and see him. I am sorry to have been a bother to you," Abigail said.

Ethan tapped his pipe on his boot heel and stood. "No bother at all. If there are two people in this world that had a right to get a look at Gideon, I figure it is me and you," he said.

"I'd be beholden to you both if you kept this to yourselves. Marcus is still jealous anytime Gideon's name comes up and God knows the fuss he would make if he found out about this," Abigail said.

Sarah stood up and patted Abigail on the back. "Don't you worry about that. Nobody else needs to know about this and if you want to see him again, you just come on over."

As Abigail rode away, Ethan watched her until she was out of sight and said, "That wasn't good was it?"

"I don't know. Seeing him was something that she had to do and maybe she has put her mind to ease now," Sarah answered.

"I don't think so," Ethan said as he headed towards the barn.

Chapter 4

Gideon was tired of dreaming. It seemed as if he had been sleeping for days, but no matter how hard he tried, he could not force his eyes open. He put Herculean effort into it to no avail. He was just too damned tired.

The dreams about Ethan had left him feeling as empty as a kicked over milk pail. He had not allowed himself to think of that time of his life in years. As far as he was concerned, Last Stand was a closed book never to be opened again. There were even dreams of Ethan's family, a wife and son named Sarah and Benjamin that talked to him. He could hear the boy talking to him now even as he tried to vanquish the dream.

He could not endure one minute more of the dreams and this time he forced his eyes open. Looking back at him was a towheaded boy with eyes and mouth so wide open that the kid must have thought he was looking at a ghost. He had seen the kid before somewhere. His mind raced trying to figure out from where he would know the child and then it all came back. He had been shot and the boy had come along and kicked his foot. As he studied him, he realized he was looking at the spitting image of Ethan Oakes thirty years ago. He wanted to curse aloud at the thought that he could ride through this place after eighteen years of avoiding it and get shot and found by Ethan's son, but instead, in a hoarse whisper, he said, "Hello, there."

"Mr. Gideon, you are awake," Benjamin said.

"Thank you for rescuing me," Gideon said.

The boy seemed to swell up at the words. His shoulders pulled back, his chest thrust out, and he grinned as if he had won a prize at the fair. "You are welcome. I'm sorry about kicking you," he said.

"Don't worry about it. You had to find out if I was alive. I expect I would be dead by now if you hadn't," Gideon said.

The boy grinned again. "I'll go get Pa. He will be so glad to see you. He has told me about you since I was a little boy," he said as he lit out of the room.

"Where are you going in such a hurry?" Sarah asked her son as he ran towards the door.

"Mr. Gideon is awake, Momma. I'm going to get Pa," he said as he disappeared out the door.

Sarah watched as Ethan and Benjamin entered the cabin and headed towards the bedroom. Ethan looked like he did the first time he was trying to get his nerve up to talk to her, and Benjamin was beside his pa, walking with purpose as if he were on a mission. "Benjamin, why don't you stay in here with me and let your pa and Gideon catch up on things. You will have plenty of time later to see him," she said.

The boy stopped and his shoulders sagged. Looking defeated, he said, "Yes, ma'am."

Ethan could feel his heart racing in his chest as he entered the room. After so many years of waiting for this day, he was not sure he was ready for it or even wanted it anymore. He had no idea on what to say. The two men locked eyes with neither seeming to have a clue on how to start a conversation. The silence grew uncomfortable.

Finally, Gideon whispered, "It's about time you tracked me down."

Ethan grinned. "You always were the better tracker," he said.

"Looks like you have done alright for yourself. That's a fine looking boy you got. He looks like he was picked from your butt," Gideon whispered.

Ethan chuckled and rubbed his cheek. "So they tell me. He's got his ma's brains though," Ethan said.

"Well, that's a good thing," Gideon said and winked.

There it was - the wink. It had been so many years that Ethan had forgotten Gideon's way of winking when he kidded you. He found it reassuring that something still remained the same.

"So how did you end up here and all shot up?" Ethan asked.

Gideon slowly inhaled a big breath before speaking. "I was working at the Chase Ranch in Cimarron when a couple of the cowhands named Bug Eye Carter and Pasty Collins decided to rustle some of the herd. They sold the cattle off and hightailed it. The fools were always talking about Silverton, and sure enough, that is where they were headed. Mr. Chase don't take kindly to cattle rustlers and sent me after them and I got careless," he said before pausing to rest. "I didn't think they were smart enough to be watching their back, but I was wrong."

"Looked like you put up a pretty good fight," Ethan said.

Gideon nodded and said, "Enough of one that they decided not to bother trying to finish me off."

"Were you going to look me up on your way through here?" Ethan asked.

Gideon looked at him blankly and then his eyelids slowly drooped shut.

Agitated, Ethan said, "You can ignore me this time, but you aren't going anywhere for a while and I will get some answers before you do."

Sarah saw the furrowed brow as soon as Ethan walked into the room. A look of frustration was what she half expected. There were too many unanswered questions for it to be perfect reunion. "How did it go?" she asked.

"Well, at least he is not an outlaw. He was chasing a couple of rustlers, though I expect that when he found them that he would have pronounced himself judge, jury, and hangman. When I asked him if he was going to stop by to visit, he conveniently went to sleep," Ethan answered.

"Be patient, Ethan. The man is just back from death's door, and besides, you know as well as me that he is not going to give you any answers that are going to make it all better or that you probably really even want to hear," Sarah said.

Ethan was looking down at the floor with his lips pursed and rubbing his thigh as if he had a Charley horse. "I know," he said and put his hat on and went outdoors.

Benjamin was sitting on the swing waiting for Ethan. "Were you happy to see Mr. Gideon, Pa?" he asked.

Benjamin's face was beaming in eager anticipation and Ethan said, "Yes, I was. It was good to talk to him again after all these years and I owe that to you. You did a fine thing, Benjamin."

His son smiled back at him as if it were the best day of his life and the mood was contagious enough that Ethan started to feel good again, letting go of his agitation. "Let's take a quick ride before supper," he said.

Sarah checked on Gideon after Ethan and Benjamin rode away. He opened his eyes at the sound of her entering the room and she could not help but notice that they were the deepest shade of blue that she had ever witnessed. He made a poor attempt to smile at her.

"Hello, Gideon. I am Sarah, Ethan's wife. I brought you some soup. How are you feeling?" Sarah said.

"Thank you for nursing me. I'm sure that it has been a burden with everything else that you have to do. As far as how I feel, well, I have had better days," Gideon whispered.

"I'm sure you have. Can you sit up some so we can get this down you?" Sarah asked.

With effort on both their parts, they managed to get another pillow behind him to prop him up. He held up his hand to stall the spoon of soup coming his way to recover from the exertion and pain. After he nodded he was ready, the spoon came at him as if the utensil was on a mission of redemption.

"Oh, my God, that is good," he said.

"Starvation probably has a way of improving the taste," Sarah said.

"So, I see Ethan didn't settle for any of these rough old cowgirls from these here parts," Gideon said.

Sarah smiled. "No, I am a Denver import," she said.

"So, did you rope him in or did he rope you?" he asked.

"Now, Gideon, you have lived long enough to know that us women always let the man think he roped us," Sarah said.

Gideon chuckled after swallowing another spoonful of soup that Sarah was shoving at him as if she were drowning out a fire. He was already starting to like her. "I bet you keep him on his toes. Ethan always did like a challenge," Gideon said.

Changing tone, Sarah said, "Gideon, I am glad that you are here no matter the circumstance. You have been an open wound ever since I met Ethan and I have no idea how all this will play out, but please remember that there is a lot of hurt bottled up in Ethan. You were like a brother that disappeared and there has never been closure. I ask that you be mindful of that when the anger comes, because it surely will,"

Gideon looked out the window and did not speak for a moment. When he spoke, his voice sounded as sad as a lone wolf howling at the moon. "I will try, but Ethan should have figured out a long time ago that some things and some people are best forgotten."

"I don't think that applies to you. Whatever your story, I know character when I see it. We all make mistakes. Now I have to go start supper. I am glad you are getting well," Sarah said as she left Gideon.

∞

Ethan and Benjamin rode in silence, reaching their pond without a word. Ethan was taking in the view when Benjamin blurted, "Mr. Gideon is running from something, isn't he, Pa?"

"No, he was chasing some cattle rustlers when they shot him," Ethan said.

"That is not what I mean. He is running from something we can't see," Benjamin said.

Ethan looked at Benjamin as if had been replaced by a miniature sage. He was not sure if he had ever realized that himself. "I expect you are right, but I doubt we will ever know what it is," he said.

"I think it was something bad that happened in the war," Benjamin said.

Ethan was impressed that his eight-year-old son had put so much thought into Gideon. Perception was a completely new side to his developing personality. "Could be. Soldiers saw more evil in one day than most men see in a lifetime. That can be hard to live with," he said.

"I'm going to try and help him," Benjamin said.

Ethan smiled at Benjamin and said, "That would be a good thing. I wouldn't ask him a lot of questions though. I don't think he would like that. Maybe just being a friend to him will help."

"Do you think I can really help him?" Benjamin asked.

"Son, I am a preacher and I believe all things are possible with God's help. Now if we don't get home for supper, we might also learn about Hell," Ethan said with a wink and then took off in a lope, leaving Benjamin giggling so hard that he had to collect himself before following after his father.

As Ethan came into view of the cabin, he could see a rider headed for their place. He recognized the gray horse as Sheriff Fuller's mount. He had been expecting him. With Doc Abram running his mouth all over town, it was just a matter of time before the sheriff showed up to check out things.

Sheriff Fuller was even older than Doc Abram. He had been around so long that he was as much a fixture of the community as the mountains. In his prime, when the territory was rough, he had held his own against the numerous outlaws and ruffians until Last Stand became a much safer place to live. This legacy gave him cache to hold onto office even though for the good of the town and his own safety, he should have hung the badge up years ago.

Putting his horse into an easy gallop, Ethan caught up with the sheriff. "Good evening, Sheriff. I been expecting you to pay us a visit," Ethan said.

"Hello, Ethan. I hear Benjamin found Gideon all shot up," the sheriff said.

"Yes, he did. Gideon is conscious now," Ethan said.

"I never thought I would ever lay eyes on him again," Sheriff Fuller said.

"Me either. He didn't plan for it to happen. Misfortune intervened," Ethan said.

Smiling, the sheriff said, "You two were full of piss and vinegar in your youth. It's a good thing I liked you boys, cause you weren't half as sneaky as you thought you were."

Ethan looked over his shoulder to see if Benjamin was in hearing distance yet. "No, sir, we probably weren't. We might have been ornery, but a least we were not mean."

"No, you were good boys," Sheriff Fuller said as they rode up to the cabin.

Gideon saw the badge when Sheriff Fuller walked into the room and recognized the sheriff immediately. It seemed unbelievable to him that the man was still sheriff. He decided that the sheriff and Doc Abram must plan to work until they died. Sheriff Fuller had once been a strapping man, but the years had left him a shell of himself and he was a bit stooped now.

"I see that I still get all classes of desperadoes showing up around here," the sheriff said and extended his hand.

Gideon shook it vigorously and said, "I don't think there are any posters out for me and they have not hung me yet."

"Tell me what happened, son," Sheriff Fuller said.

Gideon again gave the details that led him to being here. Once he was finished, the sheriff asked, "So you think these two characters are long gone then?"

"Oh, yeah. I'm sure they are in Silverton by now," Gideon said.

"Rumor has it that you done some deputying here and there over the years. That true?" the sheriff asked.

"Yes, sir," Gideon answered.

"You ought to stick around this time. I may hang this badge up one of these days," Sheriff Fuller said.

"Thank you, sir. That means a lot coming from you, but I think I have rambling disease too bad to ever settle in one place now," Gideon said.

The sheriff waved his hand in resignation and then patted Gideon's leg. "You get well, son. You hear?"

Chapter 5

"I think that I will take Gideon his breakfast this morning," Ethan said as the family finished eating eggs, biscuits, and bacon.

Grinning mischievously, Sarah said, "Help yourself, but he may be spoiled into expecting a little prettier server after these last couple of days."

"If I did not know better, I would think that you are trying to hurt my feelings. Besides, I guess until he can walk again, he will have to take whatever he gets," Ethan said with a wink.

"Pa, can I take him his supper tonight?" Benjamin asked.

"Yes, you can. Now you had better go do your chores. You know how the boss gets when the work don't suit her," Ethan said.

Gideon had improved enough to sit himself up in anticipation of breakfast. He felt more alive than dead for the first time since being shot and it lifted his spirits. "It's about damn time someone showed up to feed me. My belly has been growling ever since I smelled the bacon and eggs. You need to eat a little faster if you are going to be my waiter or feed the infirm around here first, and I prefer the waitress that works at this establishment better anyway," Gideon said.

Responding wryly, Ethan said, "You know that you could still die unexpectedly."

Ethan had spent enough time with Gideon the last few days to realize that when Gideon was relaxed, he was still the same person that he had been years ago, but at other times, there was a dark edgy person that reeked of danger. It seemed as if the two sides of his personality were in a battle to win his soul and either side could dominate at any given time.

"Yes, I could, but I feel pretty good this morning. It is kind of amazing what a little food can do for you," Gideon said.

Ethan watched as Gideon devoured the breakfast like a man starved. With his mouth full, he said, "My God, Sarah can cook. No wonder you married her."

"You should have been around here when we were first married then. It got to the point where burned food tasted normal to me," Ethan said.

Gideon chuckled. "Well, she certainly got the hang of it."

Trying to sound offhanded, Ethan said, "What are your plans when you get recovered?"

Pausing with a bite of food at his lips, Gideon said, "I have not given it any thought yet, but I suppose I will go track down Bug Eye and Pasty."

"How are you going to bring two men back to Cimarron by yourself?" Ethan asked.

Gideon looked at Ethan, pursing his lips a moment before speaking. "Ethan, I planned on making it a fight that I would win and not have to worry about bringing them back."

Ethan dropped his head and looked into his lap, contemplating Gideon's disregard for life. "I see. I kind of figured that might be it."

"You know, me and you were friends a long time ago. I am not the person that you knew then. Things change," Gideon said.

"Things do change, but I doubt people with good hearts change to bad. I think they just lose their way. What happened, Gideon?" Ethan asked.

Gideon put the bite of food down on the plate and searched the ceiling as if he were looking to find the right words to say written on it. Clearing his throat, he said, "That war was hell. There were a lot of terrible things that I did just to survive and then there was a terrible thing that I did that should not have happened – by accident. I just quit caring about much of anything after that."

"Gideon, I am a preacher now and one thing I know is that God forgives us of our sins if we are willing to accept it," Ethan said.

"You are a preacher now? Imagine that. With your conscience, I always thought that you would become one someday. I guess we really are different then," Gideon said.

"You always had one too. In fact, I remember you feeling more guilty about some of our pranks than I did," Ethan answered.

"True, but I could always see the gray between good and bad and you couldn't," Gideon said.

"You obviously have a conscience about what you did or it would not have bothered you all these years," Ethan said.

"Ethan, some things are unforgiveable. The Gideon you knew, he died a long time ago. I could not resurrect him even if I wanted. I just live my life the best I know how. I don't cause harm to anybody that don't need it," Gideon said.

"You go through life numb to feeling anything?" Ethan asked.

"I don't think about that stuff. In fact, I don't think about much of anything, I just live," Gideon said.

"I will pray for you, Gideon," Ethan said.

Gideon smiled sadly. "You do that, Ethan. I don't think God has much use for me," he said and then resumed devouring the food.

"I suppose you think it was just coincidence that you ended up getting shot here and found by my son. I think God has a plan for you," Ethan said.

Gideon did not answer for a moment as he weighed Ethan's words. "Ethan, you are the preacher and apparent philosopher, so maybe you understand the universe a whole lot better than me, but personally, I only believe in trying to live another day."

Ethan came out of the room with the empty plate and handed it to Sarah to wash. "I'm going to work on my sermon for Sunday," was all he said.

"How is our patient?" Sarah asked.

Ethan was so lost in thought that he looked at her blankly before the question soaked in. "He ate like he was starved. I think he is going to get better quickly and I'm going to make him a crutch when I am done. I don't expect he will want to stay in bed much longer," he answered.

"And how about you and him?" Sarah queried.

"I guess okay. Something happened in the war that he has been carrying around ever since then. That is the key to everything else. I don't think he will let himself be helped, but I am going to try," Ethan said.

"And your sermon?" Sarah asked.

Ethan rubbed his cheek and smiled. "Forgiving oneself," he said as there was a knock on the door.

They both looked up in surprise. Rare was the occasion when someone got to the door before they realized that company had arrived.

Ethan opened the door to find Abigail Hanson. "Hello, Abigail," he said and then stood blocking the door, unable to think of anything else to say.

From behind him, Sarah said, "Come on in, Abby. I have been expecting you."

Abigail darted in, speaking rapidly, she said, "I'm sorry to be bothering you again, but I had not heard anything new about Gideon and no knowing was making me crazy."

"He is doing much better and he is awake now," Sarah said. "Go on in there and see him."

Abby searched both of their faces trying to get a feel for what they thought about her coming. She was already guilt ridden and she wondered if they were judging her too, especially with Ethan being a preacher. It occurred to her that she was probably putting Ethan in a terrible moral quandary. "I know you probably think poorly of me for doing this, but I cannot help it," she said.

"We are not here to judge you, Abby. You are no different than Ethan in needing some closure after all these years," Sarah said. "Now, go on in there."

Abby marched into the room, not allowing herself time to think or get nervous. Gideon was sitting up, looking out the window, and the light reflected in his eyes. She noticed that they had certainly not lost any of their deep blue hue. "Hello, Gideon," she said.

He glanced quickly over at the unexpected visitor, not recognizing her. Nevertheless, something about her voice jolted his very core to the point that he could feel his scrotum drawing up. His mind raced trying to place her face.

"Gideon Johann, you do not know who I am. I guess the years have changed me too much," Abigail said.

His eyes grew large in recognition and surprise. "Hello, Abby," he said and then added by way of explanation, "When I left for the war, you were a cherub faced girl and now you are a grown woman. I guess in my mind you were still sixteen."

The thought that she would drop in for a visit had not occurred to him, though she had crossed his mind since being back. The surprise of her arrival did not give him time to decide how he even felt about it. He tried to take her appearance all in without being obvious. Even with knowing that the woman was Abby, he could not recognize the girl he had left all those years ago. Back then, she still had a little baby fat, but now the red dress that she was wearing showed off that she was a fine figured woman and pretty. Her hair had darkened to honey blond and she still had skin as smooth as a china doll. The rose had certainly blossomed and it smelled good too. Looking at her, he had a twinge of regret about what could have been.

"Yes, I am certainly all grown up now. How are you feeling?" she asked as she sat down in the chair beside the bed.

"Well, I have been better," he said with a chuckle.

She smiled and started to relax. "I guess so," she said.

"Tell me about yourself. I figured that you headed to the big city years ago," Gideon said in hopes of keeping the conversation about her.

"No, I stayed here and married Marcus Hanson and we have a daughter named Winnie that is the same age as Benjamin. I am a ranch wife much like Sarah," Abigail said.

Gideon looked out the window, annoyed that the news that she had married Marcus irritated him for some reason. He never doubted that she was a married woman, just not married to Marcus. "Just because I didn't come back didn't mean you had to settle for Marcus. You probably came to see me just to have a decent conversation," he said.

Abigail's face flushed and she said, "You conceited man. Marcus is a good man and a wonderful father. I almost became a spinster waiting around years for you to come back."

He already regretted shooting his mouth off and tried to lighten the mood, saying, "If my memory serves me well, what we did would disqualify you from being a true spinster."

Abigail's face went from flushed to peaked so fast that he knew he had made matters worse. He fingered the scar on his cheek, wishing that he could start over the whole conversation.

In a whisper, Abigail said, "Don't you ever mention that again. I only gave myself to you because you were going off to war and I wanted us to share that together in case you went off and got yourself killed. It was wrong, very wrong, and I have had to live with it ever since then."

Gideon ran his hand through his mop of hair and then rubbed the back of his neck. "I'm sorry, Abby. Marcus always was a good guy. It just caught me off-guard that you married him. He would not strike me as your type. The other thing, I was just trying to make a joke. It was a long time ago and don't matter anymore. I've never told a soul and I won't ever mention it again."

Abby turned her head away from him and looked out the window. Tears were welling up, but she was determined not to cry. It cut like a knife when he had said it did not matter anymore, leaving her wondering how she ever thought seeing Gideon would somehow bring her some peace of mind. In the silence, the clock on Benjamin's shelf that had once belonged to his grandfather seemed to grow louder with each tick as if to remind her of the time that had past. With a touch of sarcasm, she asked, "Well, now that you know about me, tell me what you have been up to the last eighteen years?"

"I've been pretty much drifting since the war. I was working on a ranch in New Mexico and was chasing a couple of rustlers for my boss when I got shot here. I've been a cowboy, deputy, and hired gun here and there until

I start feeling closed in again and then I head somewhere else. Not much to tell really," Gideon said.

"I guess with all that drifting that you never had time to write me a letter to let me know that you weren't coming back," Abigail said.

Gideon ran his hand through his hair again, silently cursing himself for getting shot around here. "Yes, Abigail, I should have written you. After the war, I did not really give a damn about anything. Still don't for that matter. And I probably was too big a coward to write you anyway," he said.

"So that war that you and your father were so hell-bent to join is the reason," she said with anger rising in her voice with each word.

"I don't want to talk about this anymore," Gideon said.

"Of course not. Like you said, it does not matter anymore. I'm sorry I bothered you. This was a huge mistake. I should have let sleeping dogs lie," she said as she stood.

"Goodbye, Abby," Gideon said.

"I hope you find some peace someday, Gideon," Abby said as she left the room.

Chapter 6

Abby's ride home did little to soothe her fury or hurt. The horse's trot felt like a substitute for a good shaking by her mother for being a foolish child and she cursed herself for acting like a silly schoolgirl running off to see her old beau. The notion now appeared unfathomable that it had ever seemed like a good idea. The thought of Gideon making a joke about her giving herself to him made her start to cry. What had been one of the most monumental moments in her life must have meant no more to him than one of the numerous whores that she was sure he had slept with over the years. She wiped her eyes and willed herself to calm down before heading down the road leading to her house.

She led her mare into the barn and found her husband, Marcus, working at repairing some tack. "Where have you been off too?" he asked.

His questioning hit her wrong as if he were being suspicious. "I just went for a ride. It's such a beautiful day. There is no crime in that, is there?" Abby said.

"Well, no there is not. I was just making conversation. What has gotten you all fired up?" Marcus asked.

"I don't ask you where you ride off to and I don't appreciate you questioning me," she said as she pulled the saddle from her horse. She brushed the mare down and put her in her stall without either of them speaking another word.

Abigail walked out to the orchard. The trees would be blooming soon and she liked to keep watch over them. She did her best thinking out here. With Gideon's return, so many things had bubbled to the surface that she needed time for reflection.

She wondered if Gideon would have been so glib about their one time together if he had known that it had produced a daughter. By the time that she realized that she was with child, Gideon was gone to war, and when she broke the news to her parents, they were mortified beyond comprehension. They refused to let her write Gideon to let him know, going so far as threatening to disown her if he learned of the baby. None of their other children had been wed with a child on the way and she would not be the first. Looking back, she knew that not writing Gideon had been a terrible mistake. In her heart, she knew that he would have come back and married her. She was just as guilty as Gideon was for the turn their lives had taken.

Her mother had a younger sister named Rita that lived in Wyoming that had never been able to bear children. Abby's parents sent her to stay with them until the child was born, telling everyone in Last Chance that Rita was bedridden with child and that Abby was going there to help out until after the child was born. She had delivered the child there. The baby was a beautiful girl with Gideon's deep blue eyes. The couple allowed her to name the baby and she had chosen Joann Marie, figuring that would be as close to giving the child her rightful name of Johann as would ever be possible. Returning to Colorado and leaving the baby was the hardest thing that she had ever done in her life. She had cried most of the way home and barely slept or ate for months afterward. The one thing that got her through that time was knowing that Aunt Rita and her husband Uncle Jake were thrilled to have a child and that Joann had a good home.

Nobody in Last Chance seemed to be any the wiser about what had really happened. After all these years, Marcus was still clueless Joann was Gideon and her daughter. There was no way possible to hide the truth in the Wyoming community and when Joann was ten, children that had heard their parents talking, started teasing her about being a bastard child, forcing her aunt to tell her the truth. The one good thing that came from the revelation was that she and Joann began writing letters. Corresponding was something that they continued to do until this day. A bond developed through the notes and Joann started spending every other summer with them. After Winnie was born, things got even better. Joann adored the child and doted on her nine year younger secret sibling.

The visits from Joann always made Abby a little nervous. She had come last summer when she was sixteen and if anybody had taken one look at her blue eyes and thought about it, they would have known that Gideon was the daddy. They were the only two people that she had ever known with such a deep blue color, but Marcus and everybody else seemed oblivious to it. Marcus was even very attached to Joann, something that Abby found amusing, knowing his dislike for anything to do with Gideon.

In her last letter to Joann, written a day after she learned of Gideon's return, she had not mentioned him, deciding to wait until she knew whether he would live or die. After her conversation with Gideon today, Abby did not see any way that good could come from Joann knowing of him coming back no matter how much the girl was curious about her father. There was no way that she could bring herself to tell Gideon that he had a daughter either. She had decided that he was too troubled of a man to add anything else to his conscience and that some things were best left alone.

She started reminiscing about all the years that she had spent waiting for Gideon until family and friends finally pushed her into realizing that she had to go on with her life. After she started seeing Marcus, she had thought that she was madly in love with him. In most every way he was the opposite of Gideon – quiet, serious, and lacking an impulsive bone in his body. It all seemed like a good thing at the time. It was not until they were wed that she realized that their courtship had been a rebound romance and that she had been more lonely than in love. Still, their marriage was not a bad one. Their union was certainly better than many couples that she knew, but it lacked the passion and playfulness that she saw in Ethan and Sarah and she longed for that.

And without Marcus, there would be no Winnie, and she could not imagine life without her. She would not change a thing about her daughter. When she was pregnant, she secretly feared that the child would be as dull as its father, but that had proven not to be the case. Winnie was full of spit and fire. She reminded Abby a lot of herself as a child with maybe even more willfulness than she had possessed. She would probably prove to be a handful when she got older, but nobody was going to walk all over her.

Winnie hollered from the back door, "Hey Momma, what are you doing out in the orchard?"

Abby looked over to see her daughter grinning at her and immediately felt better. "I'm just looking at the trees. Come out here and join me," she called out.

In a blur of skirt flying and legs and arms churning, Winnie dashed to her mother. Taking a couple of big breaths, Winnie said, "What are you looking for?"

"I just like to come out here and look at the trees. I find it very peaceful," Abby said.

Taken a tone of great importance, Winnie said, "You are not going to believe what happened to me today."

"Well, tell me then," Abby replied.

"When we were walking home from school, I was not looking, and Benjamin Oakes kissed me on the cheek and I slapped his face," Winnie said.

"Winnie," Abigail admonished.

"Well, he has no business kissing me. He can keep his lips to himself," Winnie said.

"A little kiss on the cheek is certainly not a crime. He just likes you and one of these days you might want him to kiss you and then he might be gun-shy from you hitting him," Abby said.

"Now why would I ever want Benjamin Oakes kissing on me? I ain't ever going to marry some silly boy. I'm going to live with you forever," Winnie said.

"We will see, my dear. We will see," Abby said as they started walking towards their home.

Chapter 7

"Ethan! Ethan, you need to get me a crutch or a cane and my change of clothes. I am ready to get up and move. I've had all this bed that I can take," Gideon bellowed out from the bedroom.

The family had given Gideon a wide berth since Abigail's visit. She had appeared to be upset with whatever had transpired in her reunion with Gideon and they were not anxious to find out his point of view on the subject. Ethan had finished writing his sermon and making the crutch while Sarah had busied herself with laundry.

Ethan had spent an hour in the woods looking for a tree branch long enough and with a side branch on it that could be sawed down to serve as a handgrip. He had then whittled a top for it that he bored a hole in to fit onto the branch. "I just made this today," he said, hoisting the crutch for Gideon to see as he entered the bedroom.

"Thank God. I want to be a moving target if Abby comes back. I thought that she was going to pull a Derringer out and blast me. Only a woman could stay mad for eighteen years," Gideon said.

"She has every right to shoot you," Ethan smirked.

"That may well be, but I'm sporting enough leaks at the moment. I'd prefer not to add to the collection. Did you know that she was coming, by the way?" Gideon said as he attempted to wrangle into his clothes.

Sheepishly, Ethan examined the crutch, rubbing his hand along the grain. "Uh, not really. She came and saw you while you were unconscious, but I did not know that she was coming back," he said.

"What?" Gideon shouted – his voice unusually high pitched. "You mean that she had been here before and you never thought that it was something that I needed to know?"

"I guess it just never came up," Ethan said.

"Well, I would think a married woman checking in on her old boyfriend would be news worthy. It sure would have been to me," Gideon said as wiggled into his trousers.

"I take it that it did not go well," Ethan asked.

"No, not really. You would think a married woman with a child would be past all that. That's a long time to stay mad," Gideon said.

"Gideon, you just don't understand how it felt from this side of the fence. There was never any closure with you. Your disappearance was an open wound that never healed. I felt the same way. Still do. There are times when I just want to punch you in the face for at least not writing us a letter," Ethan said.

Gideon sat silently, rubbing the scar on his cheek. "Let's see if I can walk," he finally said.

He stood using his good leg and the crutch for balance. Swaying like a pine tree, Ethan moved closer to catch him if necessary, but Gideon managed to stay upright, sucking in air as if he thought he was deflating.

"Oh, I'm light-headed," Gideon said.

"I would imagine you are still short a pint or two of blood," Ethan said.

Gideon made his first awkward steps toward the door. He face was set in determination and betrayed pain every time he put his weight on the crutch, but he seemed to limber up with each step. By the time he got to the front of the cabin, he was moving reasonably well.

"How does it feel?" Ethan asked as he stood by Gideon's side in case he still toppled.

"The leg is working better than I feared it would. The crutch makes my shoulder hurt like all get out, but it beats the hell out of lying in bed," he said.

"Do you want to go outside or do you need to sit?" Ethan asked.

"She sure is pretty these days, isn't she?" Gideon said.

"Abby?" Ethan asked, trying to follow the conversation.

"Yes, Abby. I would have thought that being married to Marcus, she would have shriveled up just from the boredom," Gideon said with a grin.

"At least some things never change," Ethan said as he followed Gideon out the door.

The day was beautiful, just warm enough to forgo a jacket and the sun felt good on Gideon face. "We had us some good times here, didn't we?" he said as he looked around the yard. "Your ma and pa were always good to me. Are they still living?"

"Yes, we did. Pa died before Benjamin was born, but Ma moved to town. She and all the other widow ladies keep themselves busy," Ethan answered.

"Sorry to hear Ben is gone. He was a good man. Why didn't your ma stay here with you?" Gideon said, walking to the well and leaning against it.

"She wouldn't hear of it. She said that she had enough of ranch life and that a young wife didn't need a mother-in-law in the way," Ethan said.

Gideon chuckled. "She always was a feisty thing," he said.

"How did you get that there scar on your cheek?" Ethan asked.

At the question, Gideon ran a finger along it. "That was how close a Reb saber came to splitting my head in two. I jerked my head back. Just ran out of room. Cutting me was the last thing that he ever did though," Gideon said.

"Oh," Ethan said, sorry that he had asked. "I bought the Johnson and Fillmore homesteads when they gave up homesteading."

"Going to be a land baron one of these days, huh?" Gideon said.

"Nah, just trying to accumulate some good land before all the free range is gone. There are more homesteaders every year. You know, there are a couple of areas with good land and water that nobody has claimed yet if you think that you would ever like to settle here," Ethan said.

Gideon studied Ethan's face, wishing that he had the goodness in him that his friend possessed. The sincerity in which Ethan had mentioned the idea of Gideon homesteading bordered on childlike naïveté. He would have laughed at the absurdity of it if not for hurting Ethan's feelings and the fact that deep down inside it made him sad that the notion was absurd. "Thanks, Ethan, but it is way too late to settle down now," he said.

"Just a thought. You know you are not too old yet," Ethan said. "When you can ride, I will show you the herd."

"I'd like that," Gideon said. "I think I'll walk around a little and try to get the hang of this."

"That sounds good. I have to ride up to the creek that feeds the pond and try to kill some beaver. They're building a dam and I'm afraid they are going to divert the water," Ethan said.

Gideon practiced with the crutch until Ethan was gone and then he headed to the barn. His tack was straddling a wall of one of the stalls and he reached in his saddlebag and pulled out the whiskey bottle. The first swallow tasted so good that he closed his eyes and let the warmth spread. He took one more swig and put the bottle back. His time here was the longest that he had gone without a drink in more years than he cared to remember. A twinge of guilt hit him for breaking his rule of only drinking at night unless in a saloon, but nothing had been normal lately anyway. He told himself that with bullet holes, and having to deal with being back home, that rules could be broken for a day. He reassured himself that on most evenings, he only took a couple of pulls from the bottle before going to sleep. It relaxed him enough to keep his mind from dwelling on the past and let him doze.

When he came out of the barn, Benjamin was sitting on the steps to the porch whittling a stick. He was so lost in his work that he did not hear Gideon approach.

"What's you doing there, Benjamin?" Gideon asked.

"Mr. Gideon, you are up and walking," Benjamin said in surprise.

"Yes, I am. All the fine care I've gotten around here has just about got me as good as new," Gideon said.

Benjamin smiled and asked, "Do you want to whittle with me?"

"Sure. Would you mind getting me my jack-knife? I saw it sitting in your room," Gideon said.

After Benjamin returned with the knife, Gideon asked, "Do you ever whittle anything but sticks?"

"Nah, I just do sticks," Benjamin said.

"I'll tell you what, if you have some pine around here for kindling, I'll show you how to make a little boat. Once you get the hang of it, we'll make us some bigger ones and then take them to the pond and sail them," Gideon said.

"Really? You'd do that with me?" Benjamin asked.

"Seems that's the least I can do for someone that saved my life," Gideon said. He got a kick out of watching Benjamin puff all up every time that he mentioned saving his life.

Gideon rummaged through the kindling pile until he found a piece of straight pine that was about two inches in diameter. He used Ethan's saw to cut a four-inch long section from it, and then using the axe, he carefully split the piece in two and handed Benjamin one of them.

"Watch me now. The first thing we do is whittle a point on one end to make the bow," Gideon instructed as he started shaving away the wood. As he worked, he kept an eye on Benjamin's progress. The boy was concentrating so hard that Gideon doubted he would even realize if he cut off a finger.

"Good work," Gideon said when the bow was finished. "Now shave the bark off to shape the sides and flatten the bottom."

As they were whittling, the roar of a Winchester rifle could be heard in the distance.

"I bet there is one less beaver in the world," Gideon said.

"Has he always been that way?" Benjamin asked.

Gideon looked at Benjamin, confused by the question. "What do you mean?" he asked.

"You know, always going after beavers," Benjamin answered.

Gideon burst out laughing. "I don't know. Let me think. You know, when we were kids, a beaver chased him one time," he said between bouts of giggles.

"I knew it," Benjamin said.

"You're a pretty sharp young man to figure that all out," Gideon said.

Benjamin smiled back at Gideon and then started whittling again. When they both had the outside of their boats shaped, Gideon showed him how to start hollowing out the inside. They were working in silence on the most challenging part of the boat when they heard footsteps behind them.

"Benjamin, it's time for you to get your chores done," Sarah said.

The boy held up his boat and said, "Momma, may I finish whittling my boat first? I'm just about finished."

Gideon watched Sarah's face and could see that she was pleasantly surprised. He wanted her to like him even though he was not quite sure why. What people thought about him was not something that ever concerned him, but she and Ethan both had a way of making him not loath himself as much as usual.

"Yes, you may, but don't make me have to come out here and remind you again," Sarah said and vanished back into the cabin.

Ten minutes passed before Benjamin announced that he was finished and proudly held the boat out for Gideon to see.

"Nice job, Benjamin," Gideon said as he examined the boat. The boy had done a better job than he was expecting for his first project. The hollowed out part was a bit rough, but not bad for an eight-year-old. "You are quite the whittler. You'll be making all kinds of things before long."

Benjamin smiled and said, "Thank you for showing me. I cannot believe that I just made this. I got to go show Momma now."

"I got a better idea. Do your chores first and then show her. That way she will be doubly pleased," Gideon said.

"You really know my momma," Benjamin said with a grin.

"No, I just know how all mommas think," Gideon said and then winked at him.

An hour later, Gideon and Benjamin were sitting out on the porch after Sarah ran them out of the cabin while she fixed supper. Ethan rode up into the yard with a beaver tied to the saddle horn. "Looks like you boys are hard at it," he said.

Grinning, Benjamin said, "We heard you massacring the beaver. Did any of them chase you?"

Ethan eyes moved slowly from Benjamin to Gideon who was grinning at him like a Cheshire cat. Trying not to smile, Ethan said, "You better worrying about me chasing you. I'm pretty sure I could whip a shot-up cowboy and a boy both at the same time. I'm going to put Pie up while you two jokers sit on your backsides loafing. After supper, you can help me skin this varmint."

Once Ethan was in the barn, Gideon said, "I didn't know that you were going to bring up the beaver chasing incident."

"If you had told me not to, I would not have, but you didn't. Besides, you know how serious Pa can be. I got to poke some fun at him sometimes for his own good," Benjamin said.

Gideon looked down into his lap, using his hat to shield his grin and said, "Oh my, boy, you are wise way beyond your years."

Chapter 8

Hank Sligo ambled up to his boss, rancher Frank DeVille. His girth made his walk out to the corral ungraceful and heavy-footed. A wardrobe of loose trousers drooping in the crotch, a wrinkled red shirt that had faded to pink, and a leather vest so stained that its original color was lost, did nothing to improve the impression. Tobacco juice dripped from the corner of his mouth and his teeth were badly yellowed from the habit began in childhood.

Migrating to Colorado after the war, Hank had been a Confederate soldier that had no desire to return to Alabama after the South's defeat. His beloved land had been laid bare by the war and he refused to be a part of rebuilding it under the North's heavy hand. He had served in General Evander Law's brigade at Gettysburg and had managed to survive the fighting all in one piece while doing his share of killing of Union troops. Considered a marksman with a rifle, he lacked the dexterity needed to have ever mastered the pistol, preferring to hide in tree lines to pickoff his quarry from long range. The carnage he had witnessed during the war had left a deep hatred for the North and its soldiers. Frank DeVille's daddy had hired the then skinny kid to work on the ranch. Back then, he could not rope and knew little of cattle, but what he lacked in experience, he more than made up for with determination. He had proved to be a quick study and over the years had worked his way up to foreman with his talent for cattle and just enough meanness to keep the men in line.

For all of Hank's bluster and brawn, women were the one thing that turned him shy and timid. He did not understand them and attempted to give them a wide berth. His only interaction was an occasional trip to the saloon where he would lay down his money for the cheapest whore they had. Even then, he got his business over with as quickly as possible and retreated back down stairs to knock back a couple more beers before heading back to the ranch.

"Have you been hearing all the gossip around town about this Gideon Johann returning home?" Hank asked in his still thick southern accent.

Annoyed that the subject had been broached, Frank said, "Yeah, I heard about it. You would think that Jesus Christ himself had returned the way everybody is going on about it."

"You know him?" Hank quizzed.

"We grew up around here together. He's a couple years younger than me. He and Ethan Oakes were always parading around like a couple of choirboys," Frank answered as he meticulously cleaned his nails with his knife and moved upwind to escape the reeking body odor of Hank.

Frank DeVille was a fastidious man when it came to his appearance. He liked to wear crisp white shirts with black trousers and if the temperature permitted, a matching black jacket. Whenever his Stetson Boss of the Plains hat began to show dirt and sweat stains, he would promptly make a trip into town to replace it and every two weeks he made the trek to Last Stand to get his hair trimmed at the barbershop. He was determined to make sure that people knew he was a man of means.

He had been on a crusade to prove that he was the most important man around ever since the day that his father's horse stepped in a gopher hole, snapping its leg and throwing the old man to the ground, breaking his neck and killing him instantly. Running the ranch was always his dream, he just never expected it under such circumstance or at so young of age. He made sure everybody knew that he was in charge as he ambitiously began expanding the size of the ranch.

"I take it there is no love lost between you two?" Hank said.

"No, we never got along much," Frank said as he watched one of his cowboys sail off a horse that they had recently bought from a questionable source. The string of animals was proving to be as wild as Indian ponies.

"I hear tell he was a blue-belly in the war, is it true?" Hank further inquired, ignoring the goings on in the corral.

"His old man and he joined up. The old man got killed and Gideon disappeared," Frank said.

"I might have to look the damn Yankee up and give him a southern welcome," Hank said.

"You best leave him alone. He could be a mean little son of a bitch in a fight before the war, and if rumor is true, he has been doing a pretty good job of it ever since," Frank said.

Hank studied his boss's face. This was the first time that he had ever seen Frank act cowed down at the mention of someone. Usually, he was ready to stomp anybody and everybody into the ground that got in his way. If he had to guess, he would say that Gideon Johann had beaten the hell out of Frank in his younger days.

All the talk of Gideon brought back bad memories for Frank. From childhood on, he had always tried to get his own way on everything. The meek may inherit the earth someday he supposed, but he planned to take all of it that he could at every opportunity. In school, he relentlessly persecuted the weaker kids until Gideon, or Ethan to a lesser extent, would interfere. Never possessing a desire for fisticuffs, he would back down before it escalated into a fight even though he towered over Gideon. One day, he got brave enough to pinch Abigail Schone on the tit when he thought no one was looking, but Gideon saw him. This time there was no stopping a fight. They were pretty much fighting to a draw until he caught Gideon with a right hook that dropped him. Seeing his chance, he dove to pin Gideon down and beat him to a pulp, but he bounced on the dirt as Gideon rolled out of the way. After that, Gideon seemed to sense that he had taken his best shot, survived, and used his quickness to beat him badly. When his old man found out what happened, he was so embarrassed to know that his son had been beaten up by the scrawny Gideon, that he had made him sleep in the barn to toughen him.

"Well, someone sure shot the hell out of him from what they are saying," Hank said.

"So they say," Frank said, wishing to conversation would end.

"You think he came back to go into ranching with Ethan? Those two together could mess with our plans for the ranch," Hank said.

"I don't think he would have showed up here all shot up if he was coming back to ranch. You tend to the cattle and ranch hands and let me worry about everything else," Frank said tersely and headed to the house.

Hank watched indignantly as the rancher walked away, befuddled that his concerns had been rebuffed so callously. Turning towards the corral, he roared, "Walter, where in the hell did you learn to ride? If you can't stay on a horse any better than that, I will find me somebody that can."

Frank walked into his house and headed straight to the liquor cabinet to pour a glass of bourbon. All the talk of the return of Gideon Johann had riled him. Not that he planned to have any encounters with Gideon, but he just brought back too many bad memories. He didn't expect the do-gooder to stay around anyway. Anybody that had been roaming that long was not likely to settle down now.

The stillness of the house still got on his nerves. He never would have guessed that he would miss the endless chatter of his wife. Back when she lived with him, all the constant talk got on his nerves so badly that sometimes he would tell her to shut the hell up, but now he found that he longed for the noise. The previous summer she had run off with one of the ranch hands. The cowboy had been so stupid that he barely could spell his name, but had somehow managed to charm his wife behind his back. She had everything that a woman could want; he let her spend generously, and she had the best clothes of all the women in Last Stand, as well as the prestige that came with being his wife. He might not have been the best husband in the world, but she could have done a lot worse.

The scandal had been deeply humiliating. He did not care if people liked him, in fact he preferred that they did not, but he did not take kindly to being the butt of a joke. He knew that the story of his wife running off had been the hottest gossip item all last summer.

He had sent Hank to track them down, but with the two thousand dollars that she had drained from their bank account, they had managed to disappear to parts unknown. He swore under his breath that he surely would have gone and killed them if Hank had found them.

He took a long sip of his bourbon as he looked out the window at the futile attempt at horse breaking in the corral. Talk of Gideon and the thoughts of his wife had put him a dour mood.

Chapter 9

The spring shower the night before had left the air smelling sweet and clean when the sun came up Saturday morning and Gideon and Benjamin were basking in it on the porch steps, whittling a set of larger boats in which they planned to attach sails. Gideon had been hobbling around for over a week on his crutch, but was still in no shape to be of any help to Ethan, and luckily for Benjamin, his father had not recruited him for any jobs yet that day.

"Make sure that you leave a high spot in the middle that we can take your pa's brace and drill a hole in it," Gideon said as he tilted his boat so that Benjamin could see how he was doing it.

"You really think we can put sails on them?" Benjamin asked.

"Well, if we don't succeed this time, we surely will in a boat or two. Just be careful and don't nick yourself. We got enough disabled slackers around here as it is," Gideon answered.

"How come Pa don't whittle?" Benjamin said.

"He used to. Running a ranch is hard. I imagine when he is not working, he is thinking about it," Gideon said.

"I wish Pa would whittle with us," Benjamin said a little wistfully.

"How come you don't have a dog? I thought all boys had a dog," Gideon asked.

"Blue died last year and I can't talk Pa into getting another one. He says it's just another mouth to feed. I don't think it's fair, but nobody listens to me," Benjamin answered.

"Your pa always had a dog growing up. He had this yellow thing he called Murphy. Murphy was so ugly that he was cute. That dog went everywhere with us. He was a good one," Gideon said as he stopped whittling and reminisced.

"That's what I figured. I'll probably be married before I get another one," Benjamin said.

Gideon grinned his crooked smile at him. "I don't know about that. If I were you, I would get a dog first and then your bride to be will know that you and the dog are a package deal. Otherwise, you might get a woman like your pa that doesn't want a dog around," he said.

"Women can be bossy, can't they?" Benjamin said.

"Whoa, don't ask me. I've never been married to one," Gideon replied.

"I heard Pa say that Miss Abigail sounded pretty mad when she visited you," Benjamin said.

Gideon made a short whistle sound. "Boy, my leg is starting to cramp. I got to get up and stretch it," he said.

He took a couple of steps, and as usual, the shoulder hurt more than the leg. "Benjamin come here and hold my crutch in case I need it. If my leg can bear weight, I don't think it could hurt any more than the crutch does my shoulder," Gideon said.

With Benjamin at his side, he took a couple of steps. He had to drag the leg, but it bore his weight. It actually did not hurt much at all; it just did not work very well. A few more steps and it loosened up a little. He made it to the well and back. It would be a good while before he was cutting the rug, but it beat the hell out of using the crutch.

"I'll be beating you in a race in no time at all," Gideon said.

"I might punch you where you got shot first," Benjamin retorted.

"Just cause you save a man's life don't mean you get to cheat," Gideon said.

Benjamin picked up his boat and started whittling again as if he was oblivious to Gideon. He was soon lost in concentration on his project. Gideon started watching a mockingbird singing up a storm when the view of the mountains caught his eye.

It had been so many years since he had lived here or even thought much about the place that he had forgotten how beautiful the area was. The mountains with their imposing snow peaks made him think of God, something that never happened. As a young man, he had always loved hunting in the woods at the base of the mountains and he had brought a lot of game back home. Fishing in the streams of blue mountain water had been one of his and Ethan's favorite pastimes. Ethan was the better angler, possessing the patience that he lacked. To top it off, the grass was some of the thickest and greenest he had seen anywhere. The land was so different from his last stop in New Mexico, where everything tended to be brown and scraggily.

He had missed out on so many things with his self-imposed exile. It had probably been ten years since he had gone fishing and now when he hunted, it was because he was running low on food, not to enjoy the peace of the woods. He tried to imagine having a family and ranch like Ethan. Both were things that he could not get his mind to envision. The idea seemed as foreign as speaking French did, though he had to admit he enjoyed the company of a kid more than he thought he could. He decided it was silly getting all nostalgic over what might have been and that he was right to have avoided this place all these years. He had chosen his course long ago and there was no going back now. Looking at Benjamin working away, he knew that it would take three slugs of whiskey to get to sleep.

That night, Gideon excused himself for his usual evening leg stretch before bed. Throughout the day he had managed to progress from dragging the leg to a pronounced limp. His limb was stiff now and getting sore from the exertion. It took all of his concentration to make the leg work as he walked around the yard. It was aching like all get out. Once it loosened up a little, he made his way to the barn, and fumbling around in the dark, he found his bottle. It felt cool and smooth in his hand.as he took his first drink. He had no reason to be in a hurry so he savored each sip until he had drunk the three swigs he had promised himself. The bottle felt about empty. He walked to barn door and held it up to the moonlight to see how much was left. There was one good drink left so he killed off the bottle. Before retreating into the barn to go put the bottle back into his saddlebag, he saw a light from the direction of the cabin coming towards him. He did not have to guess who was coming.

"Hey, Gideon," Ethan said as he walked up.

"What brings you out here?" Gideon asked.

"You know we can smell the whiskey every night when you come in," Ethan said.

Gideon's first impulse was to tell Ethan to go screw himself and mind his own business, but he just did not have it in him. The day had taken too much out of him and the whiskey was starting to make him feel mellow. "I know," was all he said.

"You want to talk about it?" Ethan asked.

In a voice that sounded monotone even to his own ears, he said, "Ethan, it's not like I'm the town drunk. I just need a couple of pops to get to sleep at night."

"Did you ever think that if you told somebody about what happened that maybe you could start to get past it? I wish that you had come to church with us. My sermon was about forgiving yourself. I guess you know that you inspired it," Ethan said.

Gideon looked down at the ground and tried to think of a good answer, but he was getting tired and his mind would not focus. Finally, he said, "I just can't talk about it. I'm too ashamed. Ethan, I know that you mean well, but let's just go to bed and forget about this. You saved my life and that is enough. You can't save my soul or teach me happiness."

They walked back to the cabin in silence. Gideon was thinking about the past again, despondent that being back had unlocked so many memories that he had buried years ago. Ethan was more convinced than ever that Gideon's return was not a random accident but part of God's plan and that he was the one to see the plan come to fruition.

When they reached the door, Ethan put his hand on Gideon's shoulder and said, "I'm glad you're back."

Chapter 10

Gideon awoke to find his clothes missing from the room and some of Ethan's apparel sitting neatly on the bed. Apparently, Sarah had decided that the time had come for his clothes to get a washing. The pants and shirtsleeves had to be rolled up just to find his hands and feet and when he fastened his belt, the waist of the trousers gathered up in clumps. Looking himself over, he laughed aloud at his appearance. He guessed the only thing worse would have been if Ethan had been a lot smaller than he was.

When Gideon came out of the room, Ethan and Benjamin were sitting at the table and Sarah was finishing frying the eggs. Sarah put her hands over her mouth to stymie a laugh, but Ethan and Benjamin roared.

"When you grow up, maybe you can fit into big boy clothes too," Ethan said between laughs, snorts, and breaths.

Gideon tried to think of a comeback, but nothing came to mind that was appropriate for a lady and child. "Whatever," he said with a smirk.

"Mr. Gideon, I could get you some of my clothes. Maybe they would fit better," Benjamin said as everybody, including Sarah, laughed now.

"I'm glad that I can bring such joy to all of you. I guess you nursed me back to health just to have something to amuse yourself with. It's a good thing you're not already eating your eggs or you would be spitting them all over each other," Gideon said as he sat down at the table.

After the teasing stopped and breakfast was finished, Gideon thanked Sarah as was his usual habit. Rising from the table, he decided that clean clothes called for a bath.

He grabbed a bar of soap and started limping to the creek. The uneven terrain made the walking hard, but it still was a joy just to be able to do it. Considering that a couple of weeks ago he had made peace with dying beside this very creek, it seemed to him to be quite a remarkable feat. The morning had put him in a good mood and spending time with Ethan and his family made him feel better about himself even if he could sense the darkness always lurking in the shadows ready to reclaim its place.

He found a sunny place where the creek pooled out of sight of the cabin that would serve the purpose for a bath. Striping, he stuck a toe in the water and yanked it back at the shock of the numbing cold. Ethan used to call him a sissy when they would go swimming and it was true that he had always hated cold water. Taking a deep breath and gathering his resolve, he walked into the water and then submerged his whole body before shooting up and gasping for air. He wondered if cleanliness was still next to Godliness if it included turning blue.

The rough soap felt good against his skin and in his hair. Even the water felt pretty good once he got used to it. Examining the bullet holes as he scrubbed, he was pleased to see that they were healing nicely with pink new skin. He would be back to good as new before long. After he finished scrubbing and sun drying, he put Ethan's clothes on and headed back.

Sarah was hanging clothes out and he walked over to her. "If you don't mind, I'm going to heat some water up and shave and when my clothes dry, I'm going to ride to town and get some new ones," he said.

"Help yourself, Gideon. Are you sure that you are ready to ride though?" Sarah asked as she continued with the laundry.

"We will see. The horse could use a ride and I'm starting to get cabin fever. Besides, if I have to wear this outfit again, I might have to shoot somebody the next time they laughed at me," Gideon answered and winked.

After shaving and getting back into his own clothes, he could pass himself off for a new man. Strapping on his gun, he checked the bullets even though he had reloaded it the day he started walking again. Out of habit, he moved the gun up and down in the holster until he was satisfied that it worked freely and then headed to the barn to saddle Buck. The horse had not been ridden since Ethan had taken him to town to get the doctor and he was feeling frisky. Buck kept moving his hindquarters away, but with some effort and a threat, Gideon got the saddle on and cinched. Mounting on the right side would have been the easy thing to do, but he was going to do it the correct way come hell or high water. He lifted his leg with his arms to get it into the stirrup and then pulling with his hands on the saddle horn for all that he was worth, the leg worked well enough to mount. Wincing and taking a big breath to drown out the pain shooting through both his leg and shoulder, he tapped his heels into the horse's ribs and started down the road.

Buck settled into an easy trot and Gideon posted to the animal's rhythm. Sitting up in the saddle, he could almost make himself believe that he was back to being his old self. He would soon have to get back on the trail of the rustlers that had shot him to finish the job he had started and settle the score. Ethan, Sarah, and Benjamin had been good to him and he was not sure how he would feel about leaving them. He already knew that it would be the first time in years that he would have some regrets about moving on. It even irked him a little to know that he could still develop feelings for people as it was something in which he did not deem himself worthy.

As he rode into Last Stand, it amused him to see that the town had not changed much at all. There were a few more houses on the outskirts, but that was about it. It still had two saloons, a couple of dry goods stores, a bank, and the other usual businesses that small towns had. None of them had even moved from their original buildings as far as he could remember.

He went into one of the dry goods store and looked around. All of the merchandise sat in the same spots as before and the store's smell of mustiness, candy, and whatever other odors that made it unique, took him back to his boyhood. He could envision himself running up to the counter with a penny to buy candy with his head barely able to see above it. Looking around, he found the clothes he needed and bought them along with some licorice. He limped out to his horse, hung his package on the saddle horn, and then headed to the telegraph office.

He sent Mr. Chase, the rancher that employed him, a brief message. "Got shot. Will finish job when can. Gideon." The telegraph operator looked him over as if he were crazy, but did not ask any questions.

His next stop was Doc Abram's office. The office was where he remembered it and when he went inside, it looked much the same as it did in his youth, just more worn, like the man sitting at his desk.

"By God, you're up and around already. Boy, you got more piss and vinegar than three normal men," Doc Abram said when Gideon walked in.

"Just good doctoring and food," Gideon said.

"That Sarah can cook, that's for sure," Doc said as he pulled off his glasses.

"I wanted to stop in to thank you and pay my bill," Gideon said.

"You know you have beat death twice now. It's time you started being more careful," Doc said.

Smiling, Gideon said, "I have to keep you in business. And besides, I hear that I make for pretty good gossip."

The doctor grinned and rubbed his chin. "That you do, my boy. That you do," he said.

Gideon paid the doctor and walked to the saloon. The name on the sign hanging on it read Last Chance Last Stand Saloon, where in the old days it had simply been Wet Whistle. He guessed somebody else ran it now. Walking in, the place was spruced up and cleaner than it used to be, but it still reeked of stale beer and smoke. The afternoon crowd, mostly cowhands, was starting to drift in and add their own note to the aroma. He could feel their eyes follow him as he sat down at a table and ordered a bottle of whiskey and a glass.

One of the two saloon girls brought the bottle on a tray and he noticed that there were two glasses on it. She was a pretty thing, petite with shiny black hair. Most of the girls that worked the saloons started looking haggard after a few years, but this one's ivory complexion and big smile would let her pass for a Sunday school teacher.

"Hey cowboy, my name is Mary. Mind if I sit down and have a drink with you?" she asked.

Gideon stood and pulled the chair out for her. As she sat, he got a whiff of her lilac perfume. She smelled like a bouquet of flowers.

"Well, aren't you a gentleman. There's not many of them around here," Mary said as she poured the whiskey into the glasses.

Gideon had noticed a huge man standing at the bar when he walked in. Now that man came lumbering towards the table. He was as tall as Ethan and weighed a good deal more. Out of habit, Gideon moved his hand under the table and checked to make sure his Colt was sliding in its holster smoothly.

"You're the legend Gideon Johann, aren't you?" he said in a heavy southern accent.

"No legend, but yes, I am Gideon," he said.

"Well you would think Jesus Christ himself had returned the way everybody is going on about you," Hank Sligo said, borrowing the line from his boss Frank DeVille.

"And you are?" Gideon asked.

"My name is Hank Sligo. I am the foreman for Frank DeVille," he said.

"What can I do for you, Mr. Sligo?" Gideon said.

"I hear tell that you were a blue-belly in the war," Hank said.

Gideon picked up his glass and looked at the whiskey's clarity before taking a sip. The place had gone stone silent and all eyes were on them. "That was a long time ago. We're all on the same side now and I try to forget about those days," he said.

Hank put his hands on the table and leaned over menacingly. "Well, I'm from Alabama and I will never forget what you blue-bellies did to the South," he said.

In a voice that was calm and quiet, Gideon said, "Hank, since you seem to know a lot about me, you probably know that I am mending from getting shot all to hell. I am in no condition to fight you and even if I was, I doubt I would stand much of a chance against a lard-ass like you, but I'm pretty sure I could put two bullets in you before those hams you call hands could touch me or your gun. So, if I were you, I would go back to the bar and mind your own business. And give my regards to Frank."

Hank remained leaning over the table, seemingly thinking what his next move would be. Finally, without saying a word, he turned and walked back to the bar as the patrons began to resume their drinking and talking. Gideon kept an eye on him until he was back to drinking his beer.

"You're a brave one," Mary said. "Hank is used to bullying his way into getting whatever he wants. That's the first time I've seen him back down to anyone."

Changing the subject, Gideon said, "How long have you lived in Last Stand?"

"My husband and I moved here about five years ago. We came here from Indiana and Eugene planned to make his fortune. We homesteaded and then the damn fool got himself killed. I didn't have any family to go back to and there is not a lot of ways for a woman to make a living around here so I turned to what I was good at doing," Mary said with wink.

Gideon sipped his whiskey. "What happened to Eugene?" he asked.

Melancholy settled on Mary's face as the question caused her to turn from telling the circumstances of her life to reliving its tragedy. She took a quick sip. "Somebody shot him out on our place. It was coldblooded murder. Eugene had picked a good homestead and I think somebody wanted it to stay open range. He was a good man and I loved him, but he didn't know what he was getting into," Mary said.

"Any ideas on who shot him?" Gideon asked.

"There's good ranchers and there are bad ones. I guess it was one of the bad ones. I don't want to speculate further than that," she said.

The conversation lagged and they both took a sip of their drink to fill the void, then Mary giggled. "Okay cowboy, tell me about the legend of Gideon Johann," she said.

Gideon rubbed his scar and smiled with a grimace. "Not much to tell. I grew up here, fought in the war, and have been wandering around the west ever since," he said.

"I know men, cowboy. You say wandered, but your eyes say you are running from some pain," Mary said.

Gideon looked at her uneasily. It made him uncomfortable that she could read him so effortlessly.

"I'm just a drifter. It's a big world out there and I like to see it," he said.

"Take me upstairs and I can make you forget that pain for a little while. I might even give you a discount for cleanliness," Mary said with a wink.

Gideon tipped back his glass and finished his drink. "I just might take you up on the offer the next time, but I need to get back."

"Suit yourself. It has been a pleasure to talk to the legend Gideon Johann. You take care," Mary said and patted his arm.

Gideon corked the bottle, stood, and tipped his hat. "Nice to meet you, Mary. See you around," he said.

With bottle in hand, he walked out into the bright light of the sun tilting to the west. He guessed it to be about three o'clock in the afternoon. A dog was barking and growling at a man that was cussing as he threw rocks at it and its pack of puppies that looked to be a couple of months old.

"Goddamn dogs are always running up and down the street. Get out of here," he yelled.

Another man walked to his horse and started to draw his rifle from its scabbard. "Old Miss Herring's damn dog has puppies every time you turn around. I'm going to put an end to it," he said.

Gideon stepped toward the man, drew his pistol, and stuck it in the man's crotch. "If you shoot that dog, I'm going to blow your balls off," he said.

"And who the hell are you?" the man asked.

"Mister, if I were you, I would be more worried about my balls than who I am," Gideon said.

The man slowly slid the rifle back into the scabbard. Gideon holstered his pistol and then quickly drew the gun again, smashing it into the man's scrotum and sending him crashing into a heap on the ground. "Nothing better happen to that dog or I will find you," Gideon said as he leaned over the man.

He turned towards where the other man had been, but he was already down the street, making a fast exit. "Does Miss Herring still live where she always did?" Gideon asked the onlookers. Someone answered that she did.

Squatting, he held out his hand and started talking to the dog. She remained wary, but the more he talked the closer she came until one of the pups bounded past her and sniffed his fingers. He scratched it under the chin and kept talking until it pressed against his knee. The mother and the rest of the pups soon followed as he petted and talked to them until they were about to knock him over with their excitement.

Picking up the first puppy, he headed to his horse with the dog in one hand and the bottle of whiskey in the other. The man he had toppled was nowhere to be seen and the onlookers had moved on down the street. Much to Gideon's chagrin, he had to ask a passerby to hold the pup while he labored to mount. Once mounted, he placed the puppy across the saddle in front of him and headed to Miss Herring's house. Thankfully, he did not have to dismount as Miss Herring was out in the yard trimming her bushes. He guessed that the woman had to be eighty-five years old. She had seemed old even back when she had been his teacher.

"Miss Herring, I don't know if you remember me or not but I am Gideon Johann," Gideon said and tipped his hat.

Miss Herring looked up and studied him. Smiling broadly, she said, "Gideon. Of course, I remember you. I am old, not senile. I heard that you had returned."

"Ma'am, I would get down and give you a proper greeting, but my leg is injured and I don't think I would be able to mount again if I did," Gideon said.

"Doctor Abram came by here and told me all about it. He said he thought you were going to die. You were a mischievous boy, but a good one and smart too. You should make something of yourself and not go around getting shot," she said.

"Well, ma'am, I did not ask to get shot," Gideon said, feeling like he was back in school.

His former teacher giggled, covering her mouth with her hands. "No, I guess you probably did not. I see you have one of my puppies there," she said.

"I heard in town that they were yours. I was wondering if I could have this one to give to Ethan Oakes' son Benjamin. He does not have one and a boy needs a dog," Gideon said.

"Ethan comes by here and sees me sometimes. You two were quite a pair," she said seemingly lost in reminiscing. A moment later she added, "I already tried to give him one of them. He would not take it."

"Miss Herring, you should know a teacher does not ask her student to do something, but tells him to do it," Gideon said.

The old woman burst out laughing and slapped her thigh. "You are correct. Go ahead and take him and don't get yourself shot anymore," she said.

Gideon tipped his hat again and rode off towards Ethan's place. On the ride back, there was nothing to do but think and the day had provided plenty of material to review. Trouble, women, and dogs made for memorable times.

Traveling as fast as he dared without jarring or scaring the puppy to death, he hoped that they would make it back to Ethan's place before supper. The pup looked uncomfortable, but he seemed to be taking it all in stride. Gideon expected a bit of a dust-up with Ethan, but one that Ethan was bound to lose.

Even though he had half-expected Benjamin to be on the step whittling, nobody was out in the yard when he arrived. It seemed a bit early, but he feared that they had started supper without him and he berated himself for dallying in town and taking a chance to miss out on one of Sarah's meals.

"Benjamin," Gideon called out.

Benjamin walked out onto the porch with Ethan behind him, drying his hands on a towel.

"We were just cleaning up for supper. Thought that maybe you were staying -. What is that?" Ethan said warily.

"Come here, Benjamin, and take this," Gideon said as he handed the puppy down to the boy.

"What are you doing bringing a dog here?" Ethan asked.

"It's a gift. Every boy needs a dog. You always had one," Gideon said offhandedly.

Irritated, Ethan said, "It is just something else to have to take care of. That should be my decision."

Benjamin was not saying anything, deciding that it was best if he stayed out of the conversation. The puppy was taking his full attention anyway, licking his face and wiggling in his arms. It was just about the cutest dog he had ever laid eyes on with its speckle white color and brown and black spots, floppy ears, and big feet.

Sarah walked out onto the porch to see what was all the commotion. Upon seeing Benjamin holding a puppy, she did her best to suppress a smile. She had lost this battle with Ethan before and did not wish to add fuel to the fire.

"Benjamin will take care of it, not you. It will be a good responsibility for him. You should be happy I brought back a boy dog instead of a girl," Gideon shot back.

Ethan seemed to grow in stature as he sucked in air and drew his shoulders back. "Oh, yes, I should be plum tickled that you took it upon yourself to decide my son needs a dog," he said.

Gideon grinned at Ethan. "That is about the size of it," he said.

Sarah took hold of Ethan's arm and laid her head against it, hoping to sugarcoat things. "Honey, you know that you have lost this one. Let it go. It will be good for Benjamin," she said.

Without another word, Ethan turned and stormed into the cabin.

Gideon was still grinning. "Should make for a pleasant supper, don't you think?" he said.

Chapter 11

Ethan was still miffed at breakfast the next morning and his conversation was curt and to the point. He barely acknowledged Gideon's presence and did not even talk to Benjamin any more than necessary. They both made a hasty retreat outdoors as soon as they finished eating while Ethan continued to give Sarah irritated looks.

"What is it?" Sarah asked. "Get it off your chest."

"You were in on this weren't you? You have been against me this whole time about not getting another dog," Ethan said.

Sarah jumped up from the table in a huff and started clearing it, banging the plates and silverware together noisily. "Listen here, Ethan Oakes, I did not know a thing about Gideon bringing a puppy home, but I am glad that he did. You were wrong not to get that boy a dog and you know it. Now if you don't wipe that scowl off of your face, I might knock it off of you," she said as she carried the plates away.

He tried not to smile, but could not help himself. Sarah was like a Banty rooster when she was stirred up and sometimes enjoying her performance was better than staying mad. "Mighty big talk for such a little lady," he said.

Still peeved, Sarah said, "You give me one more dirty look and you are going to find out it is more than talk."

Ethan stood up and pinched her on the ass. "You're awfully cute when you get all worked up," he said.

"You just get outside and get yourself busy and you can daydream about how cute I am because that is as close as you're going to get to me," Sarah said.

Ethan put on his hat and winked at her. "Yes, ma'am, but you know how dreams have a way of coming true," he said as he walked out before she had a chance to respond.

Gideon and Benjamin were working on masts for their sailboats when Ethan walked out of the cabin. Gideon looked up at Ethan, but Benjamin kept his head down avoiding eye contact.

"Do you two loafers want to ride with me to check on the herd? When we get back, you can finish your boats and go sail them if you want," Ethan said.

"Sure, we can ride with you," Gideon said.

"And Gideon, tomorrow I would like you to help me brand the new calves if you think you are up to it. See if you still know which end of the brand to grab," Ethan said.

"I think I can do that," Gideon said.

"Benjamin, you might as well bring that dog with you. We might as well get him used to seeing cattle while he is little," Ethan said and then started walking to the barn.

After he was out of hearing distance, Benjamin stood and said, "What do you think got into him?"

"Son, do not ever underestimate the power of a woman to set a man straight," Gideon said as he followed Benjamin to the barn.

They rode out with the pup sitting crossways in the saddle with Benjamin's arm hooked under his front paws. The sun was burning off the last of the morning mist but the air was still cool, making the horses frisky. Buck kept bobbing his head and fighting the bit as Gideon held him back from sprinting out in a run.

"Have you named your dog yet?" Ethan asked.

"I'm going to name him Chase. He loves to fetch my ball," Benjamin said as he rubbed the pup's head with his rein hand.

"Maybe he will retrieve birds then," Gideon said.

"Is that one of Miss Herring's?" Ethan asked.

"Yeah, I had to stop someone from shooting the momma dog yesterday. That old lady is as sharp as she ever was," Gideon said.

"Who was it?" Ethan said.

"I did not ask his name and he did not feel much like talking afterward," Gideon said.

Ethan gave him a look and Gideon grinned and said, "Don't worry, I did not shoot him or anything. I just gave him a reminder that I meant business. Speaking of surly people, who put a burr under that Hank Sligo's saddle?"

"Oh Lord, did you have a run in with him too?" Ethan asked.

"I was sitting at a table in the Last Chance and he came over and wanted to whip me. I told him I could put a couple of bullets in him before he ever touched me and he backed down," Gideon said.

"And the legend of Gideon Johann grows. You had better watch out for him. He is a mean one," Ethan said.

"Would Frank have any other kind of person work for him?" Gideon asked.

"No, probably not. Frank is the same as he ever was, always trying to bully his way through life," Ethan answered.

They rode up Pint Ridge and Ethan pulled his horse to a stop. This spot was his favorite view of the land. The mountains seemed to jut out like white haired gods with their snow covered tops and bare rock serving as craggy faces before descending to tree lines for garments and then flatting out to grass carpets. It would embarrass him to death if anybody knew how he viewed the scene.

"Gideon, in all of your travels, have you ever seen a place prettier than Colorado?" Ethan asked.

Gideon was taking in the landscape as well. "The Wyoming and Montana Territories have some great land too, but I will put home up against any of them," he said.

"That's right – home. Let's go see the cattle," Ethan said.

Crossing the valley below, Gideon got tickled watching the puppy looking around, taking everything in, as if it was the most natural thing in the world for a dog to ride a horse. They then climbed another ridge to find the cattle grazing on the other side.

"There they are. I manage them a lot different than my old man did. I cull the herd every year, getting rid of the old ones and the ones that don't produce good calves. My calves get better every year," Ethan said.

"That is a fine looking herd of cattle. You have done well," Gideon said.

"See that young bull over there. Isn't he something?" Ethan said.

"Where did you find one that nice around here?" Gideon asked.

"I spotted him at the auction in a lot of heifers and steers. Thank goodness nobody had cut him yet. I had to buy the whole pen, but I got some good cows out of it too," Ethan said.

"I don't know how good a preacher you are, but you certainly found your calling in cattle, Ethan," Gideon said.

"You can come to church with us and find that out for yourself," Ethan said.

Gideon was not listening to Ethan. His mind had drifted back to childhood memories, working with his pa on their homestead. "What happened to my parents' place?" he asked.

"Frank's daddy bought it a year or two after the war for back taxes. I tried to get Pa to buy it in case you ever came back, but you know how tight he was with spending money," Ethan said.

"Do you ever ride over there?" Gideon asked.

Ethan let out a sigh and grimaced. "It's been years, Gideon. I used to go keep up your mother's grave, but the last time I was there, Frank rode up and made such a stink, threating to have me arrested for trespassing, that I never went back. The cabin was getting pretty rough even back then," he said.

Gideon did not say anything for a moment. It had never occurred to him that his mother's grave would go unattended and he knew its neglect was his fault and nobody else. He was the one responsible and it was one more failure on his part. "Thank you for trying to keep it up. Only Frank DeVille would be such a hard ass over something like that," he said.

Ethan could think of nothing else to say about it. The condition of the grave was a sad situation that had bothered him for years with no resolution. Turning to Benjamin, he asked, "Benjamin, do you think you can keep the fire going and the brand hot for me tomorrow?"

"Yes, sir, Pa," Benjamin answered, excited with his first chance to help with the herd.

"I need to get back and work on my sermon for Sunday and then repair the corral gate," Ethan said as he turned Pie around.

After they got back, Gideon and Benjamin resumed whittling their mast poles and Ethan sat on the porch writing his sermon. They were all concentrating so hard on their work that they herd the hoof beats before they noticed the rider approaching from the west.

Rising from his seat, Ethan walked out to greet the rider and said, "Mr. Holden, I have not seen you since the spring round-up. You remember Gideon Johann don't you?"

"Sure do. Good to see you again, Gideon," Mr. Holden said as he extended his hand to him.

"What brings you over here?" Ethan asked.

"I was wondering if I could have a word with you," Mr. Holden said.

Taking the cue, Gideon said, "Ethan, I am going to take Benjamin to the barn to finish our boats. I saw some old canvas and some rawhide strips out there that I was hoping we could have if you don't mind."

"Help yourselves," Ethan said.

Mr. Holden shoved his hands into his trousers and ground a pebble into the dirt with his boot toe. He seemed uncomfortable with starting the conversation. "Ethan, after that spring round-up, I realized that I was getting too old for ranching. Since me and the misses don't have any children to take over the place, we decided we would sell it and move to town. I wanted you to have first chance at it. It's a fine homestead and decent cattle too."

"Mr. Holden, you have caught me off-guard. I never imagined you retiring or selling your place. It's a lot to think about," Ethan said.

"I know it is. I was thinking about five hundred dollars for the place and fifteen a head and five a calf. You, and Sarah, take some time and talk it over. I think that is a fair price," Mr. Holden said.

"I really appreciate you giving me first chance and it means a lot to me, Mr. Holden. You have always been a good neighbor," Ethan said.

"You have helped me way more than I've ever helped you. With your property adjoining mine, it just seemed like the right thing. Besides, we don't want Frank buying every piece of land, do we?" Mr. Holden said.

Smiling, Ethan shook the old man's hand and then watched him ride away. Climbing the steps to go talk to Sarah, he said to no one, "I'll never be able to concentrate on my sermon now."

Benjamin and Gideon emerged from the barn a short time later with sailboats in hand. With a little ingenuity, they had managed to cut the canvas into sails and bind them with rawhide strips. Mounting their still saddled horses, they headed out with their boats.

After reaching the pond, Gideon pulled the licorice from his saddlebag and handed it to Benjamin. "I forgot to give this to you yesterday after the puppy surprise went over so well with your pa," he said.

"Thank you for this and Chase. That puppy is going to be a good one, I can tell," Benjamin said as he pulled a bite off the licorice lace.

"The breeze is just about right. Let's see if they sail," Gideon said as they walked to the water.

They gave the boats a little shove and waited for the wind to catch them. Slowly the boats started moving until they were far enough from the bank that the breeze caught the sails and they picked up speed.

"By golly, I think we did it," Gideon said.

They watched in silence before Benjamin pulled off another bite of licorice and said, "Mr. Gideon, are you going to be leaving soon?"

"Yes, as soon as I am able to ride in the saddle all day, I will have to go. I have a job to finish," Gideon said.

"Will I ever see you again?" Benjamin asked.

"I don't know, maybe," Gideon answered.

"Why maybe? Can't you promise me that you will come back to see me?" Benjamin said.

"Benjamin, I never thought I would ever come back here. So, a maybe is a lot closer than I ever thought I would come, but I don't make promises that I am not sure I can keep. I do hope to see you again though," Gideon said.

"How come you don't want to move back when you finish your job?" Benjamin asked.

Gideon watched the boats and tried to think of a good way to explain things. The problem was that everything he thought of seemed insufficient until he finally gave up and started talking. "I have been drifting for so long now that I don't think I could stop even if I wanted. I get restless and have to move on. It has been good to meet you and your ma and see your pa again, but there are other things here that would remind me of what might have been," he said.

"You mean Miss Abigail don't you? Did she used to be your girlfriend?" Benjamin asked.

Gideon grinned at Benjamin. "You don't miss anything do you? Yes, Abby is what I am talking about," Gideon said.

"When I heard Momma and Pa talking about her coming by to check on you, I could tell that she was more than just an old friend," Benjamin said.

"Women are hard things to predict," Gideon said as much to himself as to Benjamin.

"I'm going to miss you," Benjamin said.

Gideon watched his boat reach the other side a couple of feet in front of Benjamin's craft. "I'm going to miss you too," he said.

Chapter 12

The day after helping Ethan brand the calves, Gideon woke up sore, but in a good mood. It had been an enjoyable day working with Ethan and Benjamin and just like the old days, it had not taken them long to get back into the swing of working as a team. With each calf, he would lasso its head to pull it from the herd and then Ethan, always the better roper, would lasso its rear legs. Ethan would then climb down from Pie to brand the calf while his horse kept the rope taut on one end and Gideon did the same on the other. Gideon could almost fool himself into believing that the last eighteen years had not happened and that they were still a couple of kids helping on the ranch. It made him ponder what might have been if they had teamed up and ranched together. He was sure that they could have been a formidable pair.

He decided that he could not go another day without tending to his mother's grave so he borrowed Ethan's wagon and harness horse to make the trip. He put everything that he could think of that he might need to repair the gravesite into the wagon, including an axe, shovel, scythe, and rake. Ethan wanted to accompany him in case there was trouble, but he would have none of it. He wanted to spend time at the grave alone. It had been way too long and he wanted to make amends.

Gideon did not see anybody about as he pulled the wagon up into what had once been their yard. A sense of melancholy settled on him as he looked around the place. So many good times and so much work were nothing but old memories now. The roof of the cabin had caved in and the porch had fallen off the front. The whole structure would soon collapse and little of the barn remained. It appeared that it been stripped of most of the lumber and what was left was rotting away. The wrought iron fence that his pa had purchased for what was to be a family cemetery was still standing and in good shape. Ethan had apparently kept it painted during the time he tended to it. The plot was so grown over with saplings and brush that he could not even see his mother's headstone.

Opening the squeaky gate to the plot, he worked his way through the growth until he got to the grave. His mother's headstone was still standing but leaning back. He could still read Martha Johann, June 4, 1826 – May 9, 1860, A Beloved Wife and Mother. Not wanting to deal with his emotions yet, he decided to clear the plot first.

The property was far enough away from Frank's place that he did not expect to be discovered, but to be cautious he kept his pistol strapped on and leaned his rifle against the fence. Grabbing the axe, he went to work on chopping down the saplings. Each blow with the axe gave his healing shoulder a stabbing pain, but the tool was sharp and most of the young trees surrendered after a few swings.

He finished cutting the saplings and was walking to the wagon to get the scythe when he saw the two riders approaching. The one man was so large that he had to be Hank Sligo and he guessed the other was Frank DeVille. He cursed under his breath. A confrontation was the last thing that he wanted to deal with at the moment. As they neared, he saw that it was indeed them. Frank had not changed much, just filled out over the years. He still looked like the bully he had always been.

They stopped in the yard, staying on their horses. "You are trespassing on my land," Frank said.

"Well, good to see you again too, Frank," Gideon said.

"You need to get out of here," Frank said.

"When I am done, I will," Gideon said.

"I could shoot you for trespassing you know," Frank said.

"Frank what makes you such a prick? When word got out that you shot me for visiting my mother's grave, it would give everybody the excuse they are looking for to hang you," Gideon said.

"I don't like you. Never have, so get off my land," Frank said.

"You can go to hell. I'm going to clean up my mother's grave," Gideon said.

Frank showed no emotion, but Hank's face scrunched up in anger and he stood up in the stirrups. "You little bastard, we may not be able to kill you, but I'm going to whip your ass," he said.

Sligo got off his horse and started marching towards Gideon. He looked like a charging goose the way he bent over with his head sticking forward to lower his center of gravity to accommodate his girth. Gideon stood his ground, waiting until Sligo was almost upon him before deftly drawing his pistol, swinging it in an arc and sending it crashing into the left side of Hank's head just above the ear. The man fell to his knees as if the hangman had dropped him from the gallows. His eyes remained open and he put his hand up to his head, but he appeared to be knocked silly.

Gideon cocked his gun and pointed it at DeVille. "Frank, I really did not want any trouble. You should have just left me alone," he said and drove his boot heel into Sligo's chest, sending him sprawling to the ground. "That is the second time your thug has threatened me. You had better get it through his head that the next time I will kill him. Now get him and get the hell out of here and leave me alone. Just remember that people that have nothing to live for are the most dangerous kind."

Frank, still showing no emotion, slowly got off his horse without saying another word, and with considerable effort pulled Sligo to his feet. Hank could barely walk and DeVille had to support him and help shove him up into the saddle. Sligo looked around blankly, apparently oblivious to his whereabouts as Frank took his reins and led him away.

Gideon grabbed the scythe and started swinging it at the brush and grass as if he could cut down every Frank Deville and Hank Sligo that had ever walked the earth. He kept up the furious pace until the cemetery plot was cleared. His arms and especially his recovering shoulder ached and he needed water, but he retrieved the rake and removed all the cuttings without taking a break. While the plot was still not restored to his complete satisfaction, the grave looked much improved and was no longer something for which to be ashamed. Exhausted, he plopped down next to the headstone and rested.

The longer he sat on the ground, the stronger the swell of words building up in him came pushing to escape. He could feel them coming almost as if he had to vomit them. "Momma, I'm so sorry I have been gone all these years and let your grave get like this. I never thought about it going unattended. I don't know why, but in my mind, your grave was being taken care of and for that, I am so sorry. I guess you know that Pa is buried in Missouri. He didn't suffer. It was real quick. I wish I could have sent him home, but it just wasn't possible. And Momma, I don't know why I thought going off to war sounded so romantic or why Pa went along with it. He should have known better. I guess he was running from the grief of losing you. We were ranchers, not soldiers. It ruined both of our lives. He was killed and I lost everything I ever cared about - Abby, this place, and any kind of life. Momma, I have to tell you something that I have never told anybody in the world.

The only people that know about it are the few that were there and they swore silence for me. There were four of us soldiers riding through the woods trying to get back to the rest of the troop. We had gotten separated during a skirmish. We were riding along and I heard this crashing noise through the brush. I thought Rebs were attacking us and I fired at the sound, and Momma, I shot a little boy right in the chest. He must have been about eight years old and I guess he was out playing. He was still alive and he was so scared. His eyes were filled with fear. I held his hand and I told him that I was sorry, but there wasn't anything we could do for him. He lived a few minutes more and then we had to leave him. We left the poor little thing out there all alone. Until this day, I don't know if his family ever found him. They still may not know what happened to him and he couldn't tell us his name. I finished out the war and have been running from it ever since. Momma, I hope you don't hate me. It was an accident and I have never forgiven myself. Some nights, I have to drink whiskey to get to sleep and forget those eyes looking up at me. Momma, I love you."

He started to cry. The tears were the first that he had shed since the night he had shot the boy in what seemed like a lifetime ago. It came upon him violently, racking his body with sobs so hard that he had to gulp for air as all the years of repression were released. After the crying stopped, he still could not forgive himself, but some of the burden felt lifted for having shared his guilt even if it had been with a grave.

Chapter 13

Gideon never bothered to tell Ethan about what happened at the gravesite, only saying that he got it cleaned up and mentioning the bad condition of the cabin. Ethan and Sarah both noticed that he had little appetite that evening and was unusually quiet and subdued around the family. That night he did not desire his whiskey and went to sleep without envisioning the dying boy's eyes staring up at him, something that seldom happened.

The next morning, he helped Ethan until lunch and then cleaned up to go to town to get some cartridges. His supply was low from the shootout and Mary was on his mind. There had been very few saloon girls in which he had ever had a decent conversation and fewer still that were pretty to boot. She was intriguing to him for sure.

As Gideon was saddling up Buck, Ethan walked out to the barn and said, "Where are you headed?"

"I need to go to town to get some cartridges," Gideon answered.

With a trace of skepticism, Ethan said, "I see."

"What? I about used up all my bullets trying to keep from getting killed. Remember?" Gideon said.

"I have a hunch that is not the bullet that you are worried about. I think you're wanting to go fire that other one," Ethan said.

Grinning at Ethan, Gideon said, "Preacher Oakes, such sinful thoughts coming from your mouth and casting dispersions on my character."

"Preacher Oakes is still a realist. Don't go getting shot," Ethan said as Gideon, still grinning at him like a fool, nodded his head and rode away.

Buck wanted to break into a full gallop and Gideon fought the reins to hold him back. This horse needed to be ridden often and for good distances or he tended to get restless and ornery. Gideon considered him a kindred spirit to love and tolerate because of it.

It would not be long before Buck would be getting all the riding he needed. Gideon knew he was close to being recovered enough to ride all day and he needed to track down Bug Eye and Pasty before they spent all their money and took off for somewhere else. On one hand, he was growing restless and ready to leave, but on the other he was dreading telling the Oakes family goodbye. He had been friendly with many cowboys over the years, but he now realized that Ethan was the only friend that he had ever had and he was going to miss the camaraderie. He had also grown very fond of Benjamin and Sarah. Benjamin was like a beacon of innocence and goodness that always brightened his day and Sarah had become a surrogate sister that he could confide in. After avoiding Last Stand all these years, he was going to have some regrets about leaving even though he expected that once he crossed the first range it would become as distant to him as it always had been.

He tied Buck up in front of the dry goods store and went in. The only person he noticed was the young man behind the counter. "I need three boxes of 44-40 cartridges and a bag of licorice," Gideon said.

As he was standing waiting to make his purchase, he felt as if he were being watched and turned to catch Abigail observing him from the corner where the bolts of material were. She quickly looked down at the material, not offering a greeting.

"I'll be back to pay for my things in a minute," Gideon said as he walked towards Abby.

"Hello Abby," he said.

"Gideon," was all she said in reply.

"Can we talk for minute?" Gideon asked her.

"I'm not sure that there is anything left to say, but suit yourself," Abby said.

Standing beside her, he wished that he had the guts to wrap her in his arms and kiss her hard on the mouth. Considering that he had been pretty much emotionless for more years than he cared to remember, he found it almost inconceivable the way feelings bubbled to the surface when he was with her. "I just wanted to tell you that I'm sorry that things turned out the way that they did. If I had it to do over again, I never would have joined the war. I expect we would be together now, but I did, and it changed me. I lost myself in that war and I am very well aware of what I lost in the process. I was a foolish young man that went off seeking adventure and my father went along with it because he was running from the grief of losing Momma," he said.

Abigail had avoided eye contact as he spoke, preferring to study the pattern of the calico material as she listened. She looked up at him and said, "Thank you for your honesty, Gideon. That was a long time ago and things happen for a reason. We were simply not meant to be."

Gideon fingered his scar and then took off his hat and ran his fingers through his hair. "There is one more thing I wanted to tell you. The time that we, uh, when you gave yourself to me, I know that the other day I made it sound like some meaningless romp in the hay and I wanted to apologize for that. That was never how I felt about it. I can't believe that I am talking about this, but I am thirty-seven years old, and I swear to you, that is the only time in my life that it ever meant anything special to me. You are the only one," he said.

Abby put her hand over her mouth and closed her eyes. "Gideon, again, thank you for your honesty. I do appreciate it, but this is so wrong. I should have never come to see you. The past should be left to gather dust. Please go," she said.

He stared at her trying to understand what he had done wrong. When he saw her standing in the corner, he had only wanted to go make things right and somehow she was as upset as the other day. His confession was likely the most honest thing that he had ever said in his life and it still seemed to do harm. He knew that she was probably right in that it all should have been avoided and there was not a damn thing that anybody could do about any of it now. "Goodbye, Abby," he said before returning to pay for his things and walking out of the store.

Abby stayed in the corner looking at material and trying to compose herself. She could not let the clerk see her upset and she just wanted to go home. To go from thinking that she was just another conquest for the only man that she had ever truly loved to knowing that she was the only person that he had ever loved was so sad and pathetic that crying was the only thing left to do. Life was not fair, never had been, and never would be and her only option was to keep marching on and not look back. It would not beat her.

Gideon placed his purchase in his saddlebags and started walking toward the saloon. As he neared it, he saw Sheriff Fuller walking toward him. "Hey Gideon, could I have word with you?" the sheriff said.

"What can I do for you, Sheriff?" Gideon asked.

"Frank DeVille came by my office yesterday and said that you were trespassing on his property and that when he asked you to leave, you knocked Hank Sligo silly. Is that the truth?" Sheriff Fuller asked.

"Well, there is a lot more to it than that. I was - ," Gideon said before the sheriff cut him short.

"Oh, I'm sure there is. That is not the part that upsets me. I have a hunch that Sligo came after you and I wanted to let you know that the next time it happens, to hit the son of a bitch hard enough to kill him," the sheriff said with a wink.

"You may get your wish yet. You take care, Sheriff," Gideon said before going into the saloon.

He sat down at the same table as his previous visit and ordered a beer. Still thinking about Abby, he decided that women had to be the most confounding thing that God had ever created. He was not even sure that he wanted to see Mary now. Abigail had certainly put a damper on his good mood. He was still confused on how one time being callous about his past with her and this time being genuinely sincere had both ended up with her upset. It seemed to him that she would have been more appreciative of his honesty. He wondered if maybe she got emotional over knowing that their past was special to him also and that the situation was all hopeless now.

Mary walked over with two beers. "Glad to see you returned, Gideon. Are you going to buy me one so I can sit here and talk to you?" she said.

He studied her face trying to decide what he wanted to do. Women did not seem to be his strong suit today or any other day for that matter, but he then concluded that maybe the only way was up from here. "By all means, join me," he said.

"I heard about you saving the dog. One more story to add to that legend," Mary teased as Gideon helped her into her seat.

"Last Stand never was a place for secrets. I wasn't about to let him kill that dog," Gideon said.

"What have you been up to?" Mary asked.

"Helping Ethan around the ranch some and teaching Benjamin how to whittle is about it," he answered.

"You look healthier than the last time that you were here, but your eyes seem to have more sadness than even before. More troubles?" she asked.

Gideon looked at her and wondered if maybe she was one of those mind readers like sometimes came around in the traveling shows. "No, nothing new," Gideon said, not bothering to tell her about his encounter with Hank Sligo or Abby.

"Maybe the healthier you feel, the more your troubles bother you then. Your eyes are easy reads," Mary said.

"Or maybe you aren't as good at reading men as you think you are. I am a restless soul, I'll admit to that, but that is about as deep as the well goes," he said before taking a swig of beer.

"Suit yourself. I'm still sure that I am right though," Mary said.

Gideon chuckled and said, "Of course, you do. You are a woman."

"When is that restless soul of yours going to need to start wandering again?" Mary asked.

"Pretty soon. I have to go track down the two men that shot me," Gideon said.

"Aren't you afraid that they might finish you off the next time?" Mary said.

"I got careless last time. I didn't think they were smart enough to know I was coming after them. I don't make the same mistake twice," Gideon said.

"Since you are leaving soon, are you going to take me upstairs this time then?" Mary asked.

"My God, you ask a lot of questions. Drink your beer and rest your tongue," Gideon said.

She smiled at him and took a sip of beer. "Did you really beat up Frank DeVille when you were younger?" she asked.

Gideon closed his eyes and shook his head in dismay. She was starting to annoy him a little now. "Yes, I planned to take you upstairs. I didn't see what the rush was, but if you are going to ask fifty questions, let's go now," he said.

She leaned over and kissed his cheek. "Don't get upset with me. It's not every day that I get to talk to a legend. Most of these cowboys around here aren't smart enough to wash off the cow shit, let alone carry on a conversation."

Gideon tipped up his beer and drained it. Reaching out his hand, she took it and led him upstairs. When he entered her room, he noticed that it was pretty much like every other brothel room that he had ever laid eyes on except that she had fixed it up a little with colorful curtains and bedspread so that it did not look so bleak. Her attempts at hominess betrayed that she should have been somebodies wife but was instead masquerading as a whore.

She sat Gideon down on the bed and then climbed behind him and started kneading his shoulders. They felt tense and she worked at getting the knots out of the muscles until his body started to go limp in relaxation, and she then started kissing the back of his neck.

"So, do you plan on making a career out of being a saloon girl?" Gideon asked.

"Well, look who's asking the questions now. I'll probably marry me a cowboy one of these days when the right one comes along. I get proposed to all the time," Mary answered.

"For love?" he asked.

"I hope it is for love. I loved Eugene, that's for sure. If I don't find love, I'll settle for a good one with a chance to make something of himself," she said.

He was so relaxed from the massage that he almost felt drunk. "You deserve to find yourself a good cowboy that you love," he said.

"Well, cowboy, I hope that I do," she said. "Now about you, what is it that you are running from?"

He was too calm to let her annoy him now, but he was tired of the subject. "What makes you so sure that I am running from anything?" he said.

"Because you don't ever quite deny it, and like I said, you are an easy read. I promise you that I always keep secrets. Get it off your chest and you will feel better. Maybe if you let it out, it won't chase you anymore," Mary said.

He could feel the secret coming up from down in the pit of his stomach. It wanted out and he wanted it out, but it got to his throat and stuck. There was no way he could tell her what had happened. His secret was an exhausting burden. He rubbed his face and let out a breath. "You are right, of course. I am running from my past, but I can't tell you about it. I just can't. It is mine to carry," he said.

Mary knew that she had lost the battle from the resolve in his voice. From the minute that she met Gideon, she had liked him even if it was obvious that he was a troubled man. Thinking that she could fix broken things was a weakness of hers. She dropped back in the bed and pulled Gideon to her. If she could not talk the pain out of him in order to heal him, she was going to love it out of him for a little while.

She thought that even his lovemaking had a sadness to it as if he could never fully let himself enjoy the moment. After they were finished, she rolled onto her side and studied his face. She could tell that she had succeeded in making the hurt go away for the time being. The lines around his eyes and brow were so relaxed that he looked like a boy. She could not help herself from studying human nature and had come to realize that good men always looked at peace afterward as if they had excised their demons for a while and bad men appeared as if the act was one more conquest in their plan to control everything in their power.

She kissed the back of his hand and then held it in both of hers. "Gideon, did you ever think about how all your running doesn't change anything or fix it? Wasting your life away won't change the past. It just makes it more of a tragedy," she said.

He smiled sadly at her. "I know all those things are true, but I just can't stop moving. It's like it catches me and gets worse whenever I stay anywhere too long. I guess it's just how I'm made," he said.

Mary dropped onto her back and pressed his hand into her breasts. She knew then that she had fallen in love with Gideon Johann, not the legend, but the troubled man that she could never have or heal.

Chapter 14

Ethan and Sarah had been debating whether to buy Mr. Holden's ranch since he had made his visit and offered it to them. Ethan was all for it and Sarah was leery of all that would be involved in taking on additional land and cattle. The previous night, they even tried to enlist Gideon in the conversation after he returned from his trip to town. He had politely excused himself and went to the barn to sip from his whiskey bottle, drinking more than usual in hope the discussion would be over by the time he returned to the cabin. Much to his chagrin, they were still arguing when he entered their home. They both gave him dirty looks when he walked in and Ethan made a snide comment about him smelling like a saloon.

Nobody was talking much at breakfast and the usual banter and teasing was nonexistent. Gideon and Benjamin exchanged knowing glances and decided the best course was to remain silent as Ethan and Sarah looked tired and in ill moods. Both of them were clearly weary of discussing the land purchase. Benjamin even excused himself to go do chores and head to school without any prompting. As soon as the meal was finished and Sarah started cleaning off the table, the debate began again.

"After looking at the numbers last night, do you feel any better about us buying it?" Ethan asked.

"Ethan, those numbers are based on your assumptions. What happens if beef prices go down? And you will have to hire a ranch hand and start paying them a wage. It is a lot to take on," Sarah said.

Gideon interrupted, saying, "I'm going to ride out and check on your herd. Hang a white flag out front if one of you surrenders, otherwise, I'm going back to where you found me and shoot myself."

"Please leave that Colt Frontier to me if you do," Ethan shot back.

Gideon strapped on the gun, grabbed his hat, and as he walked out he said, "Nah, I going to leave it to your son. You never were much of a shot with a pistol anyway."

Ethan turned his attention back to Sarah. "Honey, all your points are valid, but I really could use some help around here now and I for sure will in a year or two. I want to build a ranch big enough that Benjamin can be part of it if he wants to and not be like we were with two families trying to live off the one homestead that my pa owned. And we have done just fine with the other land that we purchased. If we do well, maybe we will be able to build a real house and get out of this cabin."

"Do you ever wish that we could have had more children?" Sarah asked.

Ethan looked at her, trying to figure out how the question had anything to do with their conversation. He realized that her random musings were one of those quirky things about his wife that made him love her. "You know I do, but I thank God every day that after three miscarriages that he gave us Benjamin. He made it all worth it," he said.

Sarah sat lost in thought before grabbing the dishtowel and waving it. "I guess I better go hang this out so that you can ride to town and see Mr. Druthers at the bank. I'm tired of talking about it and you aren't ever going to shut up until you win. You had better be right because I've seen enough calves castrated to know how to do it," she said.

Ethan grinned at her mischievously. "I really think it is a good purchase and fair value. But even if I am wrong, I am not worried about you. You couldn't live without it if you castrated me."

Sarah burst out giggling and threw the dishtowel at him. "All men think that their penis is a gift to the world," she said.

∞

The trip to town was Hank Sligo's first since Gideon had waylaid him with his pistol. He had been laid up in the bunkhouse for two days trying to get his senses back. The whole time it seemed as if his mind was in a fog and his head throbbed unmercifully. By the evening of the second day, he was so stir crazy that he decided to head to town headache or not. The beer he drank at the Last Chance seemed to work like a poultice on his head, helping him to feel better. Within an hour of buying his first, he had learned of Ethan's visit to the bank and the impending purchase of the Holden place.

With Last Stand only having two saloons, it only took drinking a beer at each place to know almost every rumor or piece of gossip in town and he liked being the ears of the operation. No bit of news was too trivial for him not to listen, giving him power to parse out what information he wanted Frank to know. Ethan's impeding purchase was certainly worthy of repeating to the boss.

∞

The next morning Hank rousted the ranch hands up early and started ragging Walter to hurry up with cooking breakfast. A lollygagging cook was not going to keep him in the bunkhouse and prevent him from being stationed on Frank's porch when his boss stepped out of the house. Once the food was cooked, Hank scarfed down his eggs and bacon, smacking loudly and slurping coffee. The others watched warily, afraid to ask the surly Sligo what the hurry was.

Hank rushed to the house and stood so close to the door that when Frank opened it, he jumped back, startled at finding the huge man filling the doorway. "What in the hell are you doing standing there? That's a good way to get knocked up the side of the head again. You could have sat on the bench like a normal person," Frank said tersely.

"I heard some big news last night. I think we need to go inside and discuss it," Hank said, ignoring Frank's irritation.

Frank studied Hank, wondering if the man sometimes thought he was part owner in the operation. He was exasperating and too familiar in his actions towards his employer to suit Frank and would have surely been fired a long time ago if he were not so essential to running the place.

Frank walked back to his study with Hank following closely at his heels. Sitting down behind his desk, he pulled a cigar out of the humidor without offering one to Hank. He clipped it carefully and then used two matches to light it while he slowly drew on it, sending large plumes of smoke into the air. Smoking the expensive cigars in front of Hank made him feel as if he established his superiority over his employee.

"Okay, what is your big news?" Frank asked.

Hank put his hands on the desk and leaned over it, too close for Frank's liking. "Ethan Oakes is buying the Holden place. He went to talk to that banker, Druthers, yesterday and got the go ahead on a loan. I'll tell you what, people think highly of Ethan. Just like this deal, Holden offers it to him without even putting it on the market. One of these days, we may all be working for him," he said.

"For Jesus Christ, Ethan doesn't have a single hired hand and I have five times the cattle that he does. He hardly qualifies as a land baron. That being said, he is the only one around here with enough brains and gumption to interfere with my plans," Frank said.

"What we need to do is start us a little range war. Kill two or three of them off and a bunch more will hightail it away from here. It might cause quite the fire sale on some land," Hank said.

"Sit down. I don't need to smell your God-awful breath. I've got a little story about range wars for you. My Uncle Joe, up in Wyoming, decided he would start him one, but he misjudged how determined his adversaries were. He only killed off one rancher, and then the rest of them, they snuck up one night and strung him up out in his own front yard. Those wars are hard things to predict and I'm sure as hell not going to start one with Gideon still around here," Frank said.

"You let me worry about Gideon. My bullet won't wound him. He will be dead before he hits the ground," Hank said.

"Yeah, I heard about how you handled him in the saloon and I saw with my own eyes how he handled you at his mother's grave. If I cowed down as easily as you did, I don't think I would talk so big if I was you," Frank said.

Learning that Frank was aware of the saloon incident agitated Hank. He nervously wiped his nose with the back of his hand and then onto his trousers. "Well, I think we ought to do something. There is less land to go around all the time and more people on the way, especially now since the Indians are about whipped," he said.

"We will wait and see what Gideon does. I expect he will be leaving soon. Doc told me that he was chasing rustlers and they ambushed him. He had no plans to come back here. Once he is gone, I got an idea on what we can do. You go run the ranch and leave me to do the thinking," Frank said and then took a big draw on his cigar and blew it towards Hank.

Chapter 15

Mary woke up at her usual time mid-morning. Sleeping in was one of the few benefits of the profession. When she had first started working at the saloon, she had had a hard time adjusting to the late nights and late mornings, but now she thrived on it. Going to bed early and rising with the chickens were about the only two things that she didn't miss about homesteading.

The homestead had been such an adventure for her and Eugene. It was as if the two of them were up against the world. They had moved to Last Stand not knowing anybody with just enough money to get started and they had managed to do most of the homesteading on their own. To their surprise, the neighbors, without asking, banded together to help them get the cabin built. It had been a wonderful gesture by the community. She even knew Ethan and Sarah back in those days.

Eugene grew up on a farm in Indiana so he had an eye for land and he picked a spot with good grass and water. His plan was to put crops on most of it and build a herd as they prospered. He used the oxen that had brought their wagon out west to plow the land up and plant their crop. The first year had gone well and they made money, but even then, they heard rumors that people were upset that they had plowed under the grass.

During the first year in the cabin, she discovered that she liked sex. Up to that point, they had lived with Eugene's parents in Indiana and it had only happened when opportunity presented itself and as quickly as possible at that. She got little enjoyment out of it. After they moved into the cabin and had the privacy to discover each other, she found that not only did she like it, but also that she was good at it. At least Eugene sure seemed to think so. They went at it like a couple of bunnies that year.

She had been raised in an orphanage, never receiving an accounting of how she ended up there. It was the only place that she could ever remember from her childhood so she assumed that she came there quite young. It certainly was not a place for nurturing, as the people there were much more likely to give out beatings than hugs. The one good thing that they did emphasize was education. Out of shear fear, the orphans learned reading, writing, and math. She had been a natural at arithmetic, much to the chagrin of the boys that were led to believe that the subject was male dominated. It was at the orphanage that she had her first sexual encounter, rape really, when one of the teachers shoved her into a broom closet and had his way with her. She had put the days of the orphanage so far in the back of her mind that she could recall very little detail about it even when she tried. The one thing besides an education that the place had given her was a refusal to let its cruelty be her nature but instead chose empathy.

The second spring when Eugene started plowing the land again is when the trouble started. At first, they found warnings nailed to trees, telling them that they needed to leave and then one night after the crops had just started to come up, somebody ran a herd of cattle across their fields. After that incident, she lost her nerve and tried to convince Eugene that they should move away. The homestead was not worth dying for she had told him, but Eugene was undaunted and replanted. Then Hank Sligo showed up at the cabin. He sat on his horse, big and menacing, and called Eugene out. They both walked out on the porch, Eugene with his shotgun. She could see him shaking trying to hold the gun steady in his arms. Hank had laughed at him and told him he was a dead man if they did not move off their homestead.

A couple of weeks later, she was hanging laundry out when she her heard the gunshot. She ran to the field and found Eugene shot in the head. The ambusher could not even kill him with some of his dignity left, but instead destroyed his face for good measure. The sheriff was sympathetic, but said there was no evidence to arrest anybody. She had no claim to the land since they had not lived on it for five years so it reverted back to open range. The only things left to do were bury Eugene, sell what few things they had, and move into the saloon.

She banished the past out of her mind and put her housecoat on to go downstairs to the back room of the saloon to make some breakfast. Mr. Vander, the saloon owner, was sitting at the table drinking coffee and going over his books.

"Good morning, Miss Mary," he said in his heavy German accent.

"Good morning, Mr. Vander," she said.

"What is wrong with my Mary these last couple of days? You have not been yourself. You fell in love with that cowboy everybody talks about, did you not?" Mr. Vander said.

She poured a cup of coffee and sat down across from him. "Maybe. I know it's a hazard of the profession and frowned upon, but he is so different from all the other men around here. He's a troubled soul, but there is a goodness to him that wants to come out," she said.

She watched Mr. Vander take a sip of coffee. He looked to be thinking hard for the right thing to say. Even though she worked as a whore for the man, she had come to love him as a father figure. He treated her as if she were one of the ladies of the town. After he discovered her math abilities, he had recruited her to help him with the books, even paying her extra for it. The old German liked to keep track of every penny coming in and going out of the place.

Mr. Vander tried to look out for his girls too. One night a bunch of rowdy cowboys from a cattle drive came into the saloon. One of the men took her upstairs and it was there that she found out that he liked it rough, blacking her eye and busting her lip. After he was finished, he grinned at her and went downstairs to play cards. She had stayed in her room nursing her wounds. Mr. Vander came up to check on her absence. He became enraged when he saw her injuries, walking her downstairs for all the patrons to see before grabbing his club from behind the bar and starting to wail away on the cowboy. One of the other cowboys drew his pistol, but before he could fire it, Mr. Vander swung the club, snapping his wrist like a twig. The man stood in shock, looking at his dangling limp and Mr. Vander swung the club again, knocking out his teeth. Nobody else dared move as he went back to beating her assaulter. If some of locals had not pulled him off, he would have killed the man.

"What you going to do about it?" Mr. Vander finally asked.

"Nothing. He will be gone soon and I'll forget about him," she said flicking a tear away and smiling sadly. "You know, sometimes life doesn't seem fair. I never set out to be a whore. If they had left us alone, I would be like all the other wives around here, having babies and going to church socials and barn dances."

"I know, Miss Mary. I know," Mr. Vander said.

Chapter 16

The full moon would be rising in a few days and Gideon decided that he would leave the next morning in order to use it to his advantage in Silverton. He had not told Ethan of his plans yet, needing to take a ride to think it all out. Saddling Buck, he rode to Ethan's pond and stood on the bank skipping rocks. He had always liked the spot and had spent countless hours fishing there with Ethan. The day was windless and the only noise was birds singing, making it a peaceful place for him and good for contemplation.

After all the years of avoiding Last Stand, he was surprised at himself for being conflicted in leaving. A part of him was ready to ride now and the other part was already longing for the place. He took inventory of all the people that had come into his life since his return. The bond with Ethan was still there after all the years, making it hard to leave the only friend he had ever had and Benjamin and Sarah had become a substitute family. Benjamin had not only saved his life, but also filled a void of the child he would never have. He would miss Mary also. She made him feel better about himself and was certainly not a run of the mill whore that deserved the hand she had been dealt. His need to always make things right pulled at him to rescue her, but he did not have a clue as to what he could do. He did not have the money to solve her problem and saw no other alternatives. Finally, he let his mind turn to the person he was avoiding thinking about – Abigail. She had been buried so far down in his past that he never thought seeing her would illicit any feelings, but there it was – he still loved her as much as he ever did and it made him feel hollow inside and a fool. He wished that he could remember why leaving her to go enlist in the army had seemed like the right thing to do. The idea seemed incomprehensible to him now and such a reckless mistake that had ruined his life. He would gladly trade the rest of his days to have that decision back and to have spent the last eighteen years with her.

Skipping one last rock across the pond, he mounted Buck. The decision was made and in the morning he would be ready to leave. All the contemplation made his head hurt. He was ready to get back to his old life and bury Last Stand in the past again. There was no way to get the last eighteen years back or fix any of it now. Being around the place just left him stuck somewhere in the middle of what could have been with all the wounds still bleeding.

At breakfast the next morning, everybody was in high spirits. Gideon and Sarah were riding Ethan about becoming a lowdown land baron and Ethan retorted with threats of finding a younger wife and a higher class of friend. At a lull in the teasing, Gideon grew serious and said, "It is time for me to get going. I'm getting out of your hair this morning."

The family all stopped mid-bite and looked at him as if he had horns growing out of his head. Ending the lull in conversation, Ethan said, "I was hoping that you would stick around and help me get the new place in shape. You could even move into the Holden place when they move to town."

"I promised Mr. Chase that I would catch Bug Eye and Pasty for him. I gave him my word and I aim to keep it. Besides, it is time Benjamin got his room back," Gideon said.

"Mr. Gideon, promise me you will come back and see me," Benjamin said.

"Benjamin, we have already gone over that. I hope to see you again one of these days, but I can't promise," Gideon said.

Sarah got up from the table and started banging pans on the stove. She could not face Gideon to say what was on her mind. "This is pure nonsense, going back out there to the life that you lived. You are too good of a person to spend your whole life drifting aimlessly and the next time when someone shoots the hell out of you, you might not be so lucky to be found. You could settle down and have a good life here. There are people here that care about you and would like to see you happy. Whatever your big Goddamn secret is that keeps you running, it is time to let it go. Only coming to terms with it will heal it, running to hell and back won't fix it," she said.

In a shocked voice, Benjamin said, "Momma."

"Hush, Benjamin," Sarah said.

Gideon stared at the egg yolk in his plate, trying to think of a response from the unexpected outburst from Sarah. "Sarah, it means the world to me that you care that much and God knows I wish it were true, but I am never going to change. Too many mistakes have been made to ever fix them now," he said.

Benjamin was about ready to cry and jumped up from the table and ran to his room, hollering, "Goodbye, Mr. Gideon."

Gideon rubbed his scar and blew out a breath. "If it means anything, getting shot was worth it just to get to be here. It was nice to learn that some things last forever, but I think it is time to go," he said as he stood up and pulled out his jackknife and placed it on the table. "Give this to Benjamin for me, please."

Sarah was staring at him now, trying to decide what else she could do before concluding that the battle was lost. She walked over and gave him a hug him and kissed his cheek. "Take care of yourself, Gideon Johann, or I will come and kill you myself," she said.

Gideon smiled and said, "You take care too."

Ethan walked out onto the porch with him. He stared out at the mountain range even though the sun reflecting off the snowcap hurt his eyes. "We're never going to see you again are we?" he asked.

"I don't know, Ethan. I just don't know," Gideon said.

Ethan hugged him and patted his back. Gideon stood rigid, caught off-guard. Hugging another man was something he had never done. Realizing that he may never see Ethan again, he hugged him back until Ethan abruptly released him and walked back in the cabin without another word. Gideon took one last look around and saw Chase. He chuckled at the memory of bringing the puppy home and then headed to the barn to saddle Buck.

Riding into town, Gideon thought about what had just transpired. Benjamin was the only one that behaved anywhere near what he would have imagined. He certainly never expected the wrath of Sarah or the hug from Ethan. As uncomfortable as it had been, it made him feel better about himself to know that others actually cared about him even as he struggled through life. He wondered if he ever confessed his secret to them if they would still feel the same way.

His first stop was at Doc Abram's office. The old doctor was sitting at his roll top desk doing paperwork when he walked in. "Good morning, Doc. I wanted to stop in and tell you goodbye. I'm heading out," Gideon said.

Doc took his glasses off and spun his chair to face Gideon. "Well, son, I'm glad I got to see you again. You made a good recovery, but you were damn lucky. You were about as close to death as you can get. How are you feeling?" he said.

"I'm almost back to good as new. The shoulder is a little weak and the leg is stiff when I first get up in the morning, but that is about it," Gideon said.

"I expect in time, they will completely heal. Muscle recovers most of the time. Will I be seeing you again?" the doctor asked.

"I can't say. Time will tell, but I don't think that it will be any time soon," Gideon said.

"Well, don't wait too damn long for I'm not going to live forever. You know the sheriff is going to die off one of these days too and you'd make a fine replacement for him. We need somebody to actually rein in some of these ranchers," Doc said.

"You'll probably outlive me. Take care, Doc," was all that Gideon said and walked out of the office.

The saloon had not opened yet. Gideon walked around to the alley and knocked on the back door. Mr. Vander opened the door, recognizing Gideon as the man in which Mary had fallen in love.

"Can I help you?" Mr. Vander asked in his stilted English.

"I'm Gideon Johann and I'm headed out and was hoping I could tell Mary goodbye," Gideon said.

"Johann, that is a good German name," Mr. Vander said.

"Yeah, my father was born there. His family moved over when he was a small boy. I never had a chance to learn the language. Pa never thought we should know it. He said we were Americans now," Gideon said.

Changing the subject, Mr. Vander said, "You know, Miss Mary is a good girl. She has had a hard life. She would make a fine wife for somebody ready to settle down and treat her right."

The forthrightness of Mr. Vander caught Gideon off-guard considering he did not even know the man. It seemed as if everybody had advice for him today and he wondered why everybody was so hell-bent on him staying in Last Stand when none of them knew what he had been up to for the last eighteen years. He could have been a bank robber for all they knew.

"I think that she would make a fine wife too. It's just that I am not the settling down type. I travel light," Gideon said.

"I see," Mr. Vander said. "Well, you are going to break her heart. I tell you that. Go on up and see her. Youth are full of foolish and folly. I tell you that."

As Gideon walked up the creaky stairs of the saloon, he smiled at the thought of being called a youth. It had been a long time since he had thought of himself as young. If this was youth, he hated to think what old age was going to be like.

Mary let him in after he woke her up on the second knock. She looked so young standing there in her nightdress with her hair messed up and sleep still showing in her face that he wondered if he was too old to be seeing her. It had never occurred to him before that she must not be any older than twenty-five

"What brings you out so early?" Mary asked warily.

"I'm heading out this morning and I wanted to stop in and tell you goodbye," Gideon said.

"Oh," she said and sat down at her vanity. "I never had one of my cowboys come by and do that."

"Well, I can't say I've ever done it before either. It was nice getting to know you and such," he said.

Mary grinned and said, "Was it the getting to know me or 'the such' that you liked the best?"

Gideon took off his hat and chuckled. "They both made me feel pretty good," he said.

Mary stood and put her arms around his neck and kissed him on the lips. "I got a little going away present for you then," she said.

Mary pulled him into the bed and took him as if her love was a fire that she wanted to spread. She tried to will him to love her and he gave back like a desperate man. What he was desperate for, she was not sure. Afterward, she held him to her as he nestled there quietly, reminding her of the babies in the orphanage that she used to cuddle to sleep.

After Gideon got up and dressed, he reached into his pocket to pull out some money and Mary grabbed his arm. "Don't you dare pay me. That was not a whore and her customer. That was a gift from one friend to the other," she said.

He kissed her awkwardly. "You take care of yourself, you hear?" he said.

"Will I ever see you again?" Mary asked.

"That seems to be the question of the day. I just don't know. I never thought I would be back and I don't know how I will feel when I get gone," Gideon said.

"Please be careful. You know I forgave whoever killed Eugene for my own peace of mind. The anger was making me a bitter person and you should forgive yourself. If I can forgive a lowlife like Hank Sligo, you can surely forgive a good man that made a mistake," she said.

"Hank Sligo killed Eugene?" Gideon asked.

"Did you hear what I said? Hank was not the point. I don't know that the killer was Hank, but he was the one that came and threatened us. The point was to forgive yourself," she said, exasperated.

"I wish I could," Gideon said. "I should have shot that son of a bitch when I had the chance."

"Just go, Gideon Johann. Just go, but know that I believe in you," she said.

He kissed her again and left. Buck was restless and so was he. Giving the horse free rein, he let him run until he slowed on his own into a trot. Silverton was a three-day ride and there was no need to wear down the horse. After an hour, he wondered why something did not feel right and smiled when he realized that it was the quiet. He had gotten used to the hustle and bustle of family life. As much as the day's outpouring had forced him to alter his opinion of himself, it had also been suffocating and the farther he rode from it the better he felt. He was back into his own element. The smell of horse sweat and the sound of creaking saddle leather were things that he loved.

Chapter 17

Business was a slow at the Last Chance Last Stand Saloon. The usual crowd had never rolled in that evening. The bartender busied himself with polishing glasses while the two saloon girls played rummy. Sligo was sitting at a table drinking a beer by himself and grumbling about the lack of company when Doc Abram walked in.

"Hey Doc, come sit with me and I'll buy you a beer," Sligo said.

The old doctor smiled as he sat down with Hank and Mary brought over the beer. He reckoned that being the town gossip had earned him more free beers than any man alive in Colorado. "Thank you, Hank. What have you been up to?" Doc Abram asked politely.

"Tending the herd. It's always busy this time of year. And yourself?" Hank said.

"I set the Thompson boy's arm today. That kid breaks a bone a year," the doctor said.

"My brother was like that, always breaking something," Sligo said. "How is that Gideon fellow doing?"

Doc took the first sip of his beer, studying Sligo's face as he did. The man was trying to act nonchalant, but his face betrayed a keen interest. The doctor decided that Sligo would never make it as an actor. "I suppose he is doing fine. He left this morning," he said.

Now Hank took a sip of his beer, not wanting to seem too anxious to inquire further. "He sure didn't stick around long. I guess that once you get that rambling in your blood, it's a hard thing to break. Do you think that he will be back any time soon?" he said.

"Nah, he said as much himself," Doc said.

"He is a strange one. As much as the people around here seem to love him, you would think he would come around more. Do you think he will ever come back?" Hank asked.

"Well, it took him eighteen years to show up this time and that was by accident, so I have my doubts," the doctor said.

"Yeah, that's kind of what I thought," Sligo said.

∞

Though Hank was bursting at the seams the next morning to tell Frank his latest news, he decided to wait until mid-morning in hopes that his boss would be more appreciative than he had been with the early morning and late evening gossip deliveries. They had ridden out to check the herd and were sitting on a ridge watching the cattle. Trying to sound offhand, Hank said, "I talked to Doc Abram in the saloon last night and he had some news on Gideon."

Frank waited for him to continue before realizing that Hank was going to make him ask. "Okay Hank, what would that be?" he said.

"Gideon is gone and he does not plan on coming back any time soon. In fact, Doc doubts that he will ever be back. That old doctor should have been a reporter the way he likes to spread the news," Hank said.

"Good. We won't have to worry about him then," Frank said.

"Do you want me to shoot Ethan like I did that whore's husband?" Hank asked.

"Hell, no, I don't want you shooting him. I already told you what happened to my uncle and Ethan has too many friends around here that would stir things up. Shooting a greenhorn is one thing, killing a pillar of the community is another," Frank said as he nudged his horse down the ridge into the herd.

"What are we going to do then?" Hank asked, riding after Frank.

"We are going to ruin him financially," Frank said.

Hank tried to get his head around what Frank meant. If the plan was to rob Ethan, it didn't seem like a good idea to him. "How are we going to do that?" he asked.

"You are going to kidnap his boy as he is walking to school. That gives you all day before anybody starts looking for him and you take him to Moccasin Cave. The things that you need to make sure of are that you surprise him and get a hood over his head so that he can't identify you and to not leave a trail to the cave. That place is so damn remote and rugged that you should be able to do it. Nobody ever rides over there unless they have cattle roam off. You do remember the place don't you?" Frank said.

"Yeah, yeah, I have been there a couple of times with you. What happens after we kidnap him?" Hand said.

"I will write a ransom note that you stick in the kid's books when you grab him. And here is the beauty of this. We will tell Jasper and Walter that all they have to do is babysit the kid in the cave and then Jasper will drop the kid off and since Walter is a little smarter, he can collect the money. We tell them that we will give them a thousand dollars apiece and they can ride off and disappear when it is all over. They aren't worth a shit as ranch hands anyway, so we won't lose much there. Those two idiots will do anything for money," Frank said.

"What if they get caught picking up the money? They would give us up in a heartbeat," Hank said.

"I got this all figured out. In the note that you leave in the book, we will tell them to go to, I don't know, maybe to Sand Creek Bridge, and then the night before they are to go there, we will leave a note on the bridge telling them to go to Sulfur Pond to leave the money. You can see for a couple of miles in every direction from there and no way that they can pull any funny business. Just to be safe, you can hide at the edge of the flats and if anybody is chasing Walter, you can kill him and we forget about the money," Frank said.

"You think we can trust Walter and Jasper to keep their mouths shut when they get drunked up in some other town down the road?" Hank asked.

Frank grinned so evilly that it gave even Hank pause. "Here is where it gets even better. Hank, you will meet them back at the cave to settle up and I want you to kill them and make it look like they killed each other over the money. Stick a hundred dollars in each of their pockets. Everybody will think that they hid the rest of it out there somewhere and will be all worried about finding it," Frank said.

"Aren't you worried that people will connect us to Jasper and Walter and wonder how they pulled it off under our nose?" Hank asked.

"We'll just tell everybody that they quit on us and told us that they were headed to Texas looking to join a cattle drive. After we get them at the cave, you can scrounge around and find us a couple of new hired hands. We'll just keep the news under our hats and keep the new guys busy on the ranch," Frank said.

"You really thought this all out didn't you?" Hank said.

"Damn right, I did. No one will ever think that we had anything to do with it and you and me will split the money. Just make sure you don't start flashing it around town. It might get you hung. Ethan won't be able to buy the Holden place and he will have to mortgage what he already owns. By the time he gets out from under that debt, I will have control of things around here," Frank said.

Chapter 18

Gideon rode for three days and was close to Silverton with plans to reach there at dusk. It had been an uneventful ride, only crossing paths with a couple of travelers. The terrain had been varied, crossing land so barren and bleak that he felt as singular as an old memory and navigating mountain ranges so glorious that he had called out just to hear the echo of his own voice, believing that maybe he did have a place in the world.

The trip provided opportunity for reflection, something that since his stay in Last Stand, he found himself doing for the first time in years. He did not intend to do it, even had hoped his life would return to normal, but found he could not avoid the contemplation. The farther he rode, the worse it got. Too many events had taken place in the last few weeks that needed sorting out and trying to make sense of what it all meant eluded him.

To his annoyance, the time with Ethan and his family had changed him. Life was much simpler before he was shot, back in a time when he never thought about anything, just lived out each day. He now realized that emotions he thought long dead were very much alive. Ethan was his brother, Sarah his sister, and Benjamin a nephew. He could even admit that he loved them no matter how foreign the emotion had become. And he loved Abby too. He knew it from the moment he heard her voice before he even recognized her face. Thoughts of her made him angry for the choices that he had made and ache with sorrow for what never could be. His feelings towards Mary confused him the most. He cared about her, but was not sure how much of it was pity. She was a good woman that had been dealt a bad hand and it collided with his natural inclination to fix wrongs.

Sarah's words about settling down, having a nice life, and coming to terms with his guilt kept running through his mind. He wondered if she was right, and if she was, how one went about forgiving oneself. The thought of forgiveness was new to him, something that he never would have even previously considered. Tired of all the contemplation, and wishing that he could quit torturing himself with all the thinking about his life, he tried to focus on the job at hand in finding Bud Eye and Pasty.

The sun was setting as Gideon neared Silverton, causing him to decide to stop for some food and take a nap until nightfall. He worried whether Bug Eye and Pasty had enough money left that they were still coming to town to blow it. Otherwise, tracking the two men down might prove hard to do. His meal was the same as every other meal on the trip, jerky and hardtack. He gulped it down before falling into a deep sleep. All the pondering on his life had left him exhausted.

When he awoke, the full moon was rising, casting shadows with its light. Riding towards Silverton, he could hear the town before he could see it. The place was loud and boisterous. Bug Eye and Pasty had always claimed that Silverton was one wild town and they apparently had not been exaggerating as he easily followed the sound to Blair Street. Over the years, he had been to many cattle towns, but never a mining town. Looking down Blair Street, he decided that Dodge City had nothing on this place. There had to be over forty saloons and brothels with enough men around to fill them. Miners were everywhere, some talking in what he believed to be German and French, while others talked in exotic sounding languages that he had never before heard. Everywhere he turned, somebody was laughing, cussing, or fighting, and up on the balconies, scantily dressed girls were calling down to the men, trying to drum up business.

He tied Buck up at the end of the street and started walking down it as anonymously as possible. There were not many cowboys in town and his dress and gun made him stand out from the miners. Everybody seemed too preoccupied with raucous behavior to pay him any mind. He realized that tracking down Bug Eye Carter and Pasty Collins was going to be difficult amongst all the crowd.

He heard a loud whistle and looked up at a balcony to see a girl dressed only in undergarments looking at him. She yelled, "Hey, cowboy, we don't get many pretty ones like you. Come on up here and I'll let you ride me bareback and you can even put your spurs to me if you like."

Gideon pulled his hat down and kept walking as the miners in the street burst out laughing and hooting. He could not help but smile even if she had brought him attention. His vanity made it hard to be upset with a whore that paid him a compliment.

Locating the horses that Bug Eye and Pasty rode seemed to be his best bet. He worked his way down the street, checking out the tied mounts. About half way down Blair, he saw a pinto and sorrel together. As he got closer, he recognized the horses and tack as their mounts. A sense of relief came over him in knowing that he would not have to track them all over the west. Now all he had to do was wait them out.

Just before midnight, Bug Eye and Pasty came stumbling out of the saloon in front of where their horses were tied. Pasty used a crutch, barely putting any weight on his right leg. Gideon had heard a scream when he held them off during the ambush, but at the time was not sure if he had hit one of them or had only sprayed him with rock chips from a shot. It looked as though he had hit Pasty pretty good.

They staggered up onto their horses and headed northwest out of town. Gideon walked back to Buck and started following them. Staying a good distance behind, he was able to keep sight of them in the moonlight. They were making so much noise singing and arguing that he probably could have ridden with them and they would have never noticed. About a mile out of town, they turned off the main trail into the woods. By the time he rode up to where they had left the path, he could see light coming from what looked to be a miner shack where they had taken up residence.

Now all Gideon had to do was wait until the following night to use the element of surprise to his advantage to make sure he took care of both of them. He found a good spot in the woods out of sight of the shack and made camp. His body was still adjusting to sleeping on hard ground again and he tossed about trying to get comfortable while thinking about how good it would be to sleep in a bed every night if he ever settled down in one spot.

The next day he kept an eye on the shack. It was close to noon before there was any sign of life when smoke started to plume from the chimney. One at a time, they ambled out, stretching and taking a piss off the front step before retreating back inside the cabin. For the rest of the day, the only times he saw them were when they answered nature calls. They appeared to be living the good life, lazing about all day and carousing at night. The day seemed like it would drag on forever for Gideon, swatting gnats and watching the place. Finally, a half-hour before sunset, they saddled their horses and rode away.

Once they were out of sight, Gideon walked to the shack and went inside. The structure was only one room with a dirt floor, cobwebs, and filth everywhere. It smelled like farts and sweat. The only things in it were two pallets, a lantern hanging by the door, and an old table with a bench. How they could spend their whole day lying around this place was beyond him. He started looking for where they hid their money, wondering if he could catch a disease touching the nasty place. If they had any left, he was sure that it had to be in the shack somewhere. Rifling through the pallets, he found nothing but dirt and bugs. The fireplace was the next logical place and he began checking each stone to see if there were any loose. He found one and began working the stone out. Stashed in the hole was one hundred and forty dollars in twenty-dollar gold pieces. He put the money in his pocket and sat down on the bench. There was nothing else left to do but more waiting.

He lost track of how many hours he sat in the dark waiting for them. His ass was so numb that it was past the point of aching and his belly growled from not eating since that morning. If he had ever experienced a longer day, he could not remember when. He was so ready to end this. When singing finally broke the silence, Gideon drew his pistol and cocked it. He had no intention of this being a fair fight.

The two men, now arguing, entered the shack and one of them struck a match and lit the lantern. As the room washed with light, Gideon said, "Good evening, boys. Good to see you again."

Bug Eye went for his gun and Gideon shot before the man even touched its grip. The bullet hit him square in the center of the chest, sending him crashing into the doorframe before sliding down in an upright position. He was not dead yet, but foam started bubbling out of his mouth and a sucking sound came from the bullet hole. Gideon cocked the gun and pointed it at Pasty, but the man did not move while encumbered with the crutch that he would have had to discard before getting to his gun.

"Bug Eye, these ambushes are not so fun, are they? Maybe if you had been better at it, you would not be dying now," Gideon taunted. He wanted to make sure the man knew his executioner.

Bug Eye's bulging eyes were already glazing over and after a couple of gurgling sounds, he stopped breathing.

"Pasty, it's your turn. Drop your crutch and draw," Gideon instructed.

"Gideon, I don't have any chance with you already aiming at me," Pasty cried out.

"It's the same chance that I had when you ambushed me," Gideon said.

"That was Bug Eye's idea. I didn't want to do it. Me and you always got along just fine," Pasty said.

"Nevertheless, you both shot me. I had three bullets in me before I even slid off my horse," Gideon said.

"Please don't shoot me," Pasty begged. "There is money hid in the fireplace. I think you have already made me a cripple for life as it is."

"I already got the money. You were a pretty good ranch hand. I don't know why you thought you had to steal," Gideon said.

"It was all Bug Eye's idea. He kept talking and talking about how easy it would be until he wore me down. He had the cattle sold before we even took them. I never stole nothing before in my life. My momma would have worn the hide off me for stealing. I went to church as a boy," Pasty said.

"Draw, Pasty," Gideon said.

Pasty dropped his crutch, standing the best he could while bearing most of his weight on his left leg. "Gideon, I am not going to draw. You can shoot me if you want, but I'm not going to cause it," he said as he slowly used his thumb and index finger to grab the butt of his gun and drop it to the floor.

Gideon watched, trying to decide what to do. In the past, Pasty would have been dead already, but now he didn't have much of a stomach for it. He suspected Pasty was telling the truth and that until Bug Eye convinced him otherwise, he had been just another honest hard-luck cowboy. The need to kill Pasty just to prove that his stay in Last Stand had not changed him waged battle against his inclination to let him go. It seemed as if his time back home had made him soft and taken away his edge that had served him so well for so long.

"Pasty, you don't know how lucky you are. I know I should kill you just to keep things nice and simple, but I'm not. How much money do you have?" Gideon said.

"Five dollars," Pasty said.

Gideon stood and reached into his pocket, pulling out two of the gold pieces and throwing them on a pallet. "I am going to Silverton and after that I'm headed back to New Mexico the same way that you two came. If I were you, I would get rid of Bug Eye and then head some other direction than the one I'm going. Find yourself another ranch to work. And don't ever make me regret that I spared you. I'll track you to hell and back if you do."

Pasty looked as if he was going to cry. He kept mopping the sweat off his brow with his sleeve. "Thank you, Gideon. And don't you worry about me. My outlaw days are over. This is as close to getting shot or hung as I ever plan to get again," he said.

"Get over on one of those pallets and stay there and don't come out of this shack until morning or I will shoot you yet," Gideon said as he picked up the two guns.

Without another word, Gideon walked outside to retrieve their rifles. He carried all the guns to the edge of the yard and left them where Pasty could find them in the morning. Exhaustion was setting in as he started making his way through the woods to Buck. The walk back seemed to be a lot farther than the trip in the morning had and when he got there, he devoured a couple pieces of hardtack and washed it down with whiskey before dropping off to sleep.

The next morning, Gideon headed to Silverton. He had no qualms over killing Bug Eye, but conflicting emotions over sparing Pasty. Moments of weakness could lead to regret or even one's own death, and besides that, he had no idea what he was going to tell Mr. Chase concerning sparing Pasty.

In Silverton, he left Buck at the livery stable and then found a decent hotel that did not double as a whorehouse. After a large breakfast, he treated himself to a hot bath and a barbered shave. Afterward, feeling like a new man, he concluded that he had done the right thing in sparing Pasty's life. He decided to stay away from Blair Street with its whores and saloons and just enjoy the day. Tomorrow would begin the long trek back to New Mexico.

Chapter 19

Frank walked into the bunkhouse just as the men were sitting down to have their breakfast. They looked up groggy eyed in surprise. The boss setting foot in their quarters was a rare occasion and even rarer when he came in not raising hell about something.

"Hank, I need to see you at the house when you get finished. Make it snappy, I got a job for you. Just come on in when you get there," Frank said before turning towards the door.

Hank had a pretty good idea what DeVille was talking about, but decided to bitch about it to make things look normal. "I wonder what damn errand he wants me to run this time," he said as he shoveled eggs into his mouth.

Sligo hurried to the house to find DeVille sitting at his desk waiting impatiently. "About time you got over here. That must have been some good eggs and bacon," Frank said.

Hank ignored the barb, and said, "What's up, Boss?"

"Today is the day. Have you got a hood to put on the kid and found a good spot to grab him?" DeVille asked.

"I got it all taken care of. Just been waiting for the word from you," Hank said.

"I'll talk to Walter and Jasper this afternoon. They should have blown most of their paycheck Saturday so that nobody will be expecting them in town any time soon. I'll send them out with a packhorse at nightfall," DeVille said.

"What happens if they aren't interested?" Hank asked as he put his hands on the desk and leaned over it.

Frank ignored Sligo's habit of getting too close. "Those dumb bastards would do anything for a thousand dollars. Don't worry about it," he said.

"You want me to stay with the kid in the cave until they get there?" Hank asked.

"Yeah, make sure you don't leave tracks. Here is the ransom note," Frank said as he handed Hank the letter.

"That shouldn't be hard to do on that rocky ground. Do you know what the kid's name is?" Hank said.

"Benjamin, I think. You better get going. You don't have much time to get over there," Frank said.

"See you tonight, Boss," Sligo said and left to saddle his horse.

Sligo rode the couple of miles to the spot where he planned to kidnap Benjamin, concealed his horse, and walked to the road. He hid behind a crop of rocks. Fifteen minutes later, he watched as Benjamin sauntered down the road. The kid looked as if he didn't have a care in the world, oblivious to his surroundings and an easy target. As Benjamin walked past the rocks, Sligo moved out from behind them and slung the hood over the boy's head without a sound. Grabbing Benjamin around the throat, he growled, "If you make a sound, I'll snap your head off like a twig."

Benjamin stood frozen, too confused to even think. He had no idea what was going on as Sligo released his grip on his neck long enough to tie the drawstring on the hood. He could see absolutely nothing through it. The huge hand returned to his throat and started walking him backwards before shoving him to the ground. A knee pinned him, pushing down so hard that he thought his chest might cave in and then his hands and feet were being bound so tightly that it felt as if the bindings were cutting through his skin. He was scared, wanting to cry, but he kept telling himself to be strong like his pa and Mr.

Gideon would be. They were the two bravest men that he knew and he would try act as he thought they would.

Satisfied that the leather strips held the boy secure, Sligo then returned to the road, stuck the note in Benjamin's books, and used a stick to cover his foot tracks. He then threw the boy over his shoulder and started walking to his horse. The animal was hid about a hundred yards away, and as he walked, he zigzagged to stay on rocky ground. By the time he made it back to his mount, he was winded and his shirt was sweat stained from the effort. He threw Benjamin across the saddle horn and mounted.

"Just keep your mouth shut and you will come out of this unharmed. We have a bit of a ride in front of us. Do you understand?" Hank said.

"Yes, sir," Benjamin said while nodding his head.

Benjamin recognized that they were traveling a rocky trail from the clack of the horse hoofs and the jarring that felt as if the saddle horn was going to push through his belly and out his back. It made it hard to breathe and he was dizzy from hanging with his head pointed towards the ground. He was at a loss as to why he had been taken or what would happen to him. Even though the man that took him made sure that he did not get a look at him, Benjamin recognized the southern accent the moment he spoke. He did not know his name, only that he was the man that worked for Frank DeVille, but he decided that he would keep that to himself or it might get him killed.

Sligo finally arrived with Benjamin at Moccasin Cave. Taking rocky paths to the cave had made the trip a lot longer and his ass felt as if it were rubbed raw from being pressed tightly against the cantle because of the space the kid was taking. He led the horse into the mouth of the cave, pulled Benjamin off the saddle and sat him against the wall where the light shone in. "I've got to go gather

some wood. You sit tight and don't make me shoot you,"
he said.

∞

Sarah had started preparing supper when Ethan
walked in from working all day moving the cattle to fresh
grass. "Your son is not home from school yet. When he
walks through that door, I'm going to tan his britches, and
don't you try to stop it," she said.

"I haven't unsaddled Pie yet, maybe I better ride out
and check on him," Ethan said.

"I'm sure he is just lollygagging down the road. You
know how he gets," Sarah said.

Ethan rode out expecting to find Benjamin just down
the road. Seeing no sign of him, he put the horse into a
trot. He was starting to grow concerned. Benjamin was
never this tardy. A half mile from the cabin, he saw the
books and lunch pail lying in the road. Climbing down
from his horse and picking up the pail, he felt the weight
of the lunch still inside it. Foreboding ran through him
before he even saw the note sticking out between the
books. It read, *"Mr. and Mrs. Oakes, We have kidnapped
your son and are holding him for $5000.00 ransom. Take
the money in $20.00 gold pieces to Sand Creek Bridge on
Saturday noon. No harm will come to your son if you follow
out instructions."*

The burden of the news forced Ethan to squat and
inhale large breaths of air to fight off faintness. As he tried
to reread the letter, it trembled in his shaky hands as if he
had palsy and his vision was obstructed by blackness on
the edges of his periphery. Kidnappings were something
that happened out east, never around here that he had
ever heard. His mind raced to try to think of possible

culprits, but fear for Benjamin's safety made it impossible to concentrate.

He put Pie in a gallop towards home. Breaking the news to Sarah was going to be the hardest thing that he had ever done in his life and he was not sure that she was strong enough to endure another heartbreak. It seemed inconceivably cruel that after all the years that Sarah and he had tried to have a child to have him snatched away by evil. He wondered how God could let such a thing happen.

Sarah was standing with her hands on her hips ready to pounce when they walked through the door until Ethan came in carrying the pail and books, looking white as a sheet. "Oh, my God, what has happened?" she asked.

Ethan held out the note in front of her. "Somebody kidnapped him. It happened this morning, his lunch is not eaten," he said.

Sarah dropped into a chair and read the note, looking up at Ethan when she was done. "What kind of person would do this and why?" she asked in a voice so pitiful that Ethan had to steel himself not to cry.

"I don't know. I can't think right now, it just gets all jumbled up in my head. Can you ride to town to tell the sheriff? I will go back and try to find some tracks. We'll run out of daylight if we wait for the sheriff to get back from town," Ethan said.

Sarah stood and put her arms around Ethan, resting her head against his chest. "What are we going to do if you can't find him? He's just a little boy," she said and started to cry.

"I don't know, Sarah, I really don't. I'll saddle a horse for you. We have to get busy. There's no time to waste," he said as he stroked her head and kissed her.

Looking up at her husband, Sarah said, "Ethan, find my baby."

∞

As the sun started to set in the west, Hank Sligo lit one the torches he had left in the cave when scouting things out the previous day. Legend had it that the first time a white man had explored the cave, he had found six pair of moccasins lined up together. No one ever came up with a good explanation for the moccasins being left there, but the name stuck. Pieces of pottery were still lying around along with some markings on the walls and some people claimed that the cavern was haunted by an Indian ghost. It had a fresh water supply where a spring trickled out of the cave wall and made a pool before running deeper into the cave. Frank had once told him that some men had followed the stream a mile in and the cave still kept on going, but they had enough exploring and headed back out. The area with the pool was like a great room that made a right turn from the entrance, allowing a fire without fear of being spotted from the mouth and yet close enough that it would draw out the smoke.

Throwing Benjamin over his shoulder, he carried him to the great room where he had made the woodpile and started the fire. He dropped him to his feet before cutting the biddings off the boy's hands and feet. "If you so much as touch that hood to scratch your nose I'm going to shoot you. Just sit still," he said.

"Why did you take me?" Benjamin asked.

"We are holding you for a ransom. Do you know what that is?" Hank asked.

"Yes, sir, but my pa ain't got no money," he said.

Sligo chuckled. "He has land and cattle and can turn that into money," he said.

"Why are you doing this?" Benjamin asked again.

"Just hush, boy. If you do what you are told, everything will be fine. You'll get to go home and we will get the money. In case you are wondering, you are in a cave. I have to go to the mouth of it and wait. You just sit still. If you go in deeper, nobody will ever find you and you will die, and if you try to sneak out, I will shoot you, so just sit," Sligo said as he pushed Benjamin down onto his rear before walking away.

Sligo waited impatiently at the cave entrance, watching Jasper and Walter finally ride up in the moonlight. "Glad to see you boys could make it," he said sarcastically.

"Frank made us go the long way, avoiding the roads to get here. It's no picnic in the dark," Jasper said.

"The kid is inside. I don't have him tied up right now and you can take the hood off him. It won't matter that he sees you. You all will be long gone when this is over with. Tie him up when you go to sleep," Sligo said.

"Frank laid it all out for us," Walter said.

"Just make sure you don't mention any of our names. All you have to do is babysit and keep an eye on him. And you better feed him tonight too. He hasn't had anything all day," Hank said.

Jasper giggled and said, "We're going to be rich."

"Yes, we are. So don't screw it up. Take your horses in the cave and get your supplies unloaded so that I can get headed back with the packhorse. There's a pool of water in there," Sligo said.

"When are you coming back?" Jasper asked.

"I don't know yet, so don't get trigger happy if you hear me coming. No fires during the day. I don't want smoke billowing out of the mouth like an Indian sending up smoke signals. In the morning, make sure that there are no tracks outside and then keep your asses in there," Sligo said.

∞

Ethan searched the area around the spot that he had found Benjamin's books and pail until it became too dark to see. He had started the search frantically scurrying about looking for something obvious until calming down and methodically covering the area. During his search, he came to the realization that the kidnapping was well planned and that he would not be able to track them. He could feel the bile rising up into his throat at the thought that he had no idea in the world where to look for his son. As he stood there worrying about Benjamin, Sarah and Sheriff Fuller rode up.

"Did you find anything, Ethan?" Sheriff Fuller asked.

"No, somebody planned this out well. The ground is so rocky around here that there is no way to find tracks," Ethan said.

"In all my years of sheriffing, I've dealt with about everything that you can think of, but never a kidnapping. I'll get a search party up tomorrow and we'll scour the whole damn countryside," he said.

"That's a lot of territory to cover. Whoever did this will have a good hiding place," Ethan said.

Sarah sat on her horse with her hands covering her face. "What are we going to do, Ethan?" she asked.

"I've been thinking that I need to go talk to Mr. Holden and tell him that we cannot buy his place and then go to the bank and see if they will let us mortgage our place. With everything paid for, I pray that they will go along with it," Ethan said.

"This is really happening isn't it?" Sarah said.

"Why would anybody single out us?" Ethan said as much to himself as to the others.

Chapter 20

Ethan and Sarah spent the evening sitting at the kitchen table trying to talk their anxieties away and holding hands while praying. They discussed the kidnapping until they were merely repeating themselves and when the mantle clock chimed twelve times, they decided it best to try to surrender to sleep. The endeavor proved largely useless as they slept fitfully, waking each other up with their tossing and turning, and gladly arising at the first sign of dawn.

Neither Ethan nor Sarah had an appetite for breakfast, preferring black coffee in hopes of washing away their exhaustion. Both had dark circles under their eyes and their faces were puffy from lack of sleep. Sarah could not sit still, jumping up every few minutes and pacing before returning and sitting back down at the table.

"I better head over to see Mr. Holden and tell him what happened and then head to the bank. We need to know if they will lend us the money," Ethan said.

"What are we going to do if they refuse?" Sarah asked.

"Our land and cattle are worth a lot more than five thousand dollars. I think they will go along with it. It would be bad for business to turn us down," Ethan said.

"He's just a little boy, Ethan. Imagine what he must be going through. He must be so scared," Sarah said.

"I know, Hon. I thought about that all night, but he's brave and he's smart. We have to have faith in Benjamin too," he said.

"All the miscarriages were bad, but they were nothing compared to this," she said and started crying.

He tried to hug her from behind the best that he could with her sitting with her head down on the table. "We have to have faith that the Lord will get us through this and return Benjamin to us," he whispered in her ear.

"I know, but it's not fair. We've lost enough children," she said.

"I've got to go. I'm going to find the sheriff after I go to the bank and help him with the search. I hate to leave you here all alone, but we don't have much choice," Ethan said.

"I'll be fine. Find my boy, Ethan," Sarah said.

As he rode to see Mr. Holden, Ethan wished that Gideon were around. Sarah and he had both gotten accustomed to his company and missed him. He doubted that Gideon would have been able to do anything more than was being done, but it would have been nice for them to have him to lean on and he was sure that Gideon would have left no stone unturned in trying to find Benjamin

Mr. Holden was sitting on his porch when he arrived. "Sit down and smoke a pipe with me, Ethan. Do we have a closing date yet?" he said.

Ethan climbed off his horse and sat down beside the old man. "Mr. Holden, something terrible has happened. Somebody has kidnapped Benjamin and is holding him for ransom. I won't be able to buy your place. I'm going to have to mortgage everything I own to pay them," he said.

"Those lowdown sons of a bitching bastards," Mr. Holden said as he hopped up and started walking back and forth on the porch.

The outburst was the first time that Ethan had ever heard his neighbor swear and was afraid that the old man was so worked up that he would have a stroke. "Calm down, Mr. Holden. We don't need you getting sick over this. Sheriff Fuller is looking for them now," he said.

"This happened because you were going to buy this place," Mr. Holden said.

Ethan looked at him as if he were speaking in tongues. The idea of land being behind the kidnapping had not occurred to him. "Oh, surely nobody around here would steal my son over land," he said.

"Ethan, I know you are a preacher and look for the good in people, but don't think for a minute that some of the ranchers around here are not upset over you buying my place and the timing sure seems peculiar. Never underestimate the depths to which a greedy man will stoop," he said.

"Mr. Holden, are you okay with me backing out on you," Ethan asked.

"Why of course, my boy. You have to do what is best for your family. I'll just take the damn place off the market until the sheriff gets to the bottom of this. I can ranch another year if need be," Mr. Holden said as he held out his hand to shake with Ethan.

"Thank you, Mr. Holden. I have to get to town. God bless you," Ethan said before riding away.

Ethan pondered whether Mr. Holden could be onto something or if it probably was an old man's imagination running wild. He knew that one of his own weaknesses was a penchant for being naïve, but he had a hard time suspecting his fellow ranchers. Some of them were not particularly nice men, but none that he knew of was considered a criminal either.

He constantly scanned the horizon in all directions hoping to see something out of place, but things looked the same as they always did. The snow was retreating down the mountains a little every time he checked and the wildflowers were in full bloom. He wondered where in all that vastness was his son.

A meeting with Mr. Druthers at the bank was never an enjoyable experience. The little bald man was devoid of any sense of humor or personal skills. He would peer out over the top of his spectacles with his thin-lipped mouth clenched so tightly that it looked more like a crack in his face, seemingly enjoying that he held a customer's fate in his hands. "What can I do for you today, Mr. Oakes?" he said.

"I don't know if you have heard about what happened to my son or not," Ethan began.

"Yes, yes, of course. It was all the talk of the town this morning when word got out that Sheriff Fuller was recruiting a search party. I am very sorry for you and your family," Mr. Druthers said.

Ethan played with his hat in his hands, working his fingers around the brim. "I talked to Mr. Holden today and he released me from our sales agreement. So I won't be needing a loan for that, but I need to mortgage our place to raise the five thousand dollar ransom," he said.

"So you want to mortgage your four hundred and ninety-five acres and your cattle herd. Loaning you the money on the new acquisition was one thing, because you would still have all the other to fall back on, but loaning you money against your entire operation would leave you no reserves if we would have a harsh winter that decimated your herd or the bottom fell out of beef prices. It would leave the bank quite vulnerable," Mr. Druthers said.

"Mr. Druthers, we are talking about my son here, not some whimsy I just came up with," Ethan said.

"Yes, yes of course. I am not unsympathetic to your plight, but I am charged with safeguarding the bank's resources," the banker said.

"I am as safe of a risk as any man around and you know it. True, we could have a bad winter or prices could bottom out, but they would have to be extreme to prevent me from making payments on a ten year note," Ethan said.

"True, true. I just need some time to think about this," Mr. Druthers said.

Ethan slammed his palm down on the banker's desk. "I don't have time. I have to have five thousand dollars in twenty-dollar gold pieces by Saturday. How long do you think this bank will last after word gets out that my son died because you would not loan me the money. I would bet people will start pulling their money out the Monday after my sermon on the evils of banks," Ethan said.

Mr. Druthers peered at Ethan over his glasses and scratched his nose. "A succinct point, Mr. Oakes. When do you need the money?" he asked.

"Before noon Saturday," Ethan said.

"Very well. I will have to make sure that I procure enough gold pieces. Meet me here at nine in the morning Saturday and I will have it ready. You can sign the papers then. Good day and I hope they find your son," Mr. Druthers said.

"Thank you," Ethan said before leaving.

Ethan walked out of the bank wanting to hit something. He wondered if the banker realized how close he had come to getting the snot beaten out of him. Bankers were one notch above outlaws in his book. The main difference was that their robbing was legal and nobody got shot.

He looked around for the sheriff and learned that he had already headed out to start the search. The sheriff had rounded up some volunteers first thing that morning, sending them out to the ranches for additional help, and was having everybody convene at the spot Benjamin had been kidnapped. With his business finished, Ethan climbed up on Pie to head out to help them.

∞

Sarah was sitting out on the porch getting some fresh air. After Ethan left, nerves had gotten the better of her and she had been vomiting since then. She was near hysterical worrying about Benjamin, trying to imagine what he was going through and whether he was still alive. Her imagination had gotten the better of her as she let her mind drift to dark thoughts where she assumed the worst.

The three miscarriages had been hard. They had left her barely motivated to get out of bed and with so little appetite that she became painfully thin. She questioned her faith, her ability to bear children, and her fitness as a wife. Each time she managed to snap out of it in a couple of months, but after the third loss, she gave up on ever having children. When she realized that she was pregnant with Benjamin, she did not allow herself the joy of being an expectant mother until she made it to the fourth month. By then she was showing and knew that this baby had the will to live. It had been a wonderful time for her and Ethan. To now have somebody cruelly snatch that joy away was worse than anything she could imagine.

Sarah could see someone coming in a lope and new instantly that the rider was Abby from the skirt billowing on each side. She rode up into the yard, jumping off the horse like a man, and marched towards Sarah, giving her a hug as Sarah stood to greet her.

"Sarah, I am so sorry that this has happened. I am here for you for whatever you need and Marcus is out helping with the search. Do you have any news?" Abby said while still embracing Sarah.

"No, nothing new. Ethan went to talk to the bank and then help with the search," Sarah said as they sat back down on the swing.

"I can't believe this is happening in our little community. What kind of people takes a child?" Abby said.

"I don't know, Abby. I've been wondering if kidnapping Benjamin was random or we were targeted. Did we do something to cause this?" Sarah said and started crying.

Abby took Sarah's hand. "If you were targeted, it wasn't that you did anything wrong, but because they want to ruin you," she said.

"Do you think this happened because we were going to buy the Holden place?" Sarah asked.

"I don't know. Some of these ranchers are son of a bitches, but I don't know that they would stoop to this. I don't think even Frank DeVille is mean enough or has enough guts for kidnapping," Abby said.

"I feel so helpless. My poor baby is out there all by himself and he must be scared out of his mind. And God knows what they might be doing to him," Sarah said.

Abby feared that they would never see Benjamin alive again, but she was not about to dash Sarah's hopes. "I think that they will take care of him. They want money and to get away with it. The law will be looking for them a lot harder if they do harm to Benjamin," she said.

"I hope you're right. I'm so worried that I can't think straight," Sarah said.

"Maybe the search party will find them today," Abby said, trying to stay positive.

"I don't know. Ethan looked last night until dark at the spot that they took him and could not find any tracks. They knew how to cover themselves and this is an awfully big place to search," Sarah said.

"Gideon knows how to track. That's what he was doing when he was shot, wasn't it?" Abby said.

"Abby, Gideon left last Thursday," Sarah said. She could see that her words caught Abby off-guard and upset her even as she tried to hide it. It would be easy to judge her for being married and having feelings for another man, but she understood that there had never been the usual closure and that his reappearance had reopened wounds that had been festering for years. In her mind, Abby was just human.

"That figures. Never around when you need him," Abby said.

"He'd be here if he knew about it and you know it," Sarah said a little defensively.

Sarah's words gave Abby an epiphany. "If they don't have any success today, I'm going to find Gideon," she said.

Sarah looked at her in surprise. "Abigail, what could Gideon do that the sheriff or Ethan and the rest of the men could not? And how in the world do you think you could find him?" she asked.

"Sheriff Fuller is a good man and was a good sheriff, but he has no business riding a horse these days let alone being a sheriff. And Ethan and Marcus and all of the rest of the men around here are ranchers, farmers, and cowboys. Gideon fought in a war and has been a deputy and a hired gun. We need him here," Abby said.

Sarah sat thinking about what Abby had said. Her points were valid though she hoped it would not come to needing Gideon's expertise. "He went to Silverton. That is a three day ride and the ransom is due on Saturday," she said.

"If he is still there, then it will be too late, but I bet he is headed this direction on his way back to New Mexico. God knows he will avoid this place like the plague if he doesn't know that he is needed," Abby said.

"Marcus would never allow you to go after him," Sarah said.

"Marcus doesn't tell me what I can and can't do and I am the logical choice. You and Ethan need to be here and I don't trust Marcus to make a real effort to find Gideon. I've never seen a man so jealous over on old boyfriend, and besides, I can ride as well as any man. I was a pretty good cowhand for Dad and Marcus before I had Winnie," Abby said.

The mention of Winnie had started Sarah worrying about Benjamin again. "My poor Benjamin," she said.

"I'm going to go make you some of that tea that we both like," Abby said.

∞

Ethan found the sheriff directing the volunteers in a search for tracks at the sight of the kidnapping. There were about twenty men that included town people, ranchers, or the ranch hands sent in their place. Looking out at the bunch from his saddle, Ethan did not feel hopeful. If Hank Sligo's stories were to be believed, he was the only one searching that probably had any real experience in tracking. It surprised him that Frank had bothered to send him.

"Hello, Sheriff. Has anybody found anything?" Ethan asked.

"No, not yet. I telegraphed the U.S. Marshal and got word back that he has a posse out chasing Charles Allison. Looks like we are on our own," the sheriff said.

Ethan climbed off his horse and walked up to the sheriff. "They knew how to not leave tracks, didn't they? Have you come up with any ideas on who might have done it?" Ethan asked.

"Yeah, they did. Everybody I can think of that might stoop to this, I don't think is smart enough to be this careful," he said.

"That's me too. Mr. Holden thought it could be one of the ranchers upset that I was buying his place, but I can't imagine any of them taking such a risk just to prevent me from buying a piece of land," Ethan said.

"I thought of that, but I agree with you. We've never had any troubles except when that whore's husband was killed, but I never was sure that there wasn't more to that story after she chose her new profession," Sheriff Fuller said.

Ethan let the remark pass as Mary was a source of guilt for him. He had liked the couple when he had gotten to know them and felt as if he and the community had let her down after Eugene was killed. He did not have any ideas on who killed Eugene, but he was sure that Mary had not done it. "I'll get started helping," he said.

The volunteers searched a quarter mile in all directions until noon when they regrouped and took a break. The men were grumpy and frustrated with their lack of success and a couple of them seemed as if they were ready to give up and go home.

Sheriff Fuller decided he needed to take charge of the situation before there was any more complaining. "Alright, boys, here is what we are going to do. We divide up into four groups and each group will head in a different direction, widening out as you go. Check barns, abandoned shacks, caves, whatever could hide somebody. If you see something, wait until we get back here and can go in as a group. Everybody meet back here at five," he said and started grouping the men.

Hank Sligo determined that it would be an advantageous time to run his mouth. Frank had decided it would look good to have him help and would keep them in the loop on what the sheriff was thinking. "I'd like to find the bastard that took the boy. Any man that steals a kid should be hung," he said.

"Just remember that is for the court to decide. We are here to find Benjamin first and foremost," the sheriff said. "Now let's ride."

∞

Walter had spent most of the morning talking with Benjamin. He liked the kid and was doing his best to keep him calm, promising him that he would get to go home on Saturday. They had moved to the front chamber of the cave for the natural light. Walter and Benjamin sat with their backs to the cave wall while Jasper, always restless, paced and got on Walter's nerves.

Jasper stuck his head out the cave and saw a rider headed towards the cave. "Quick, get the kid back in the dark. Somebody is coming," he said as he took his hat and started covering footprints. "And kid, if you make a sound, Walter will blow your brains out. I think it is your pa and I will kill him the second that you make a sound."

Walter carried Benjamin into the dark chamber, pulling his gun so that the boy could feel it pressed against his chest as he held him. Jasper finished covering the tracks, found the horses in the dark, and started petting them, ready to hold their heads to keep the bits from rattling.

The rider was actually Abby's husband Marcus. He rode up to the mouth of the cave, dismounted, and drew his gun as a precaution. Walking around, he saw no sign that anybody had been there before entering the cave and inspecting the floor further. He lacked matches to go any farther in, but stood listening until satisfied that the cave was empty before leaving.

After Jasper was certain that the rider was gone, he moved to the front of the cave and peered out. "Damn, that was close. It's okay now, bring the boy back out," he said.

"They must have a search party out looking for us. That should be the end of them coming up here," Walter said as he set Benjamin down and holstered his pistol.

Benjamin covered his face and started to cry. The gun held against him and the fear that his pa was about to die had unnerved him. He just wanted to go home and see his momma and pa. If he ever got home again, he promised himself that he would never misbehave again.

"Quit your crying, you little baby," Jasper said in his agitated state.

∞

The men started straggling back to the kidnap spot a little before five o'clock. The men were a dejected bunch of searchers, having found nothing. The sheriff questioned them about the places they had checked while Sligo listened intently. When Marcus mentioned Moccasin Cave, he almost swallowed his tobacco and looked around quickly to see if anybody was watching him. Fortunately for him, all eyes were watching Marcus.

"Ethan, I don't know what else to do. We have covered a lot of territory and going out any farther would be like a needle in a haystack. I think you better plan on paying the ransom," Sheriff Fuller said.

Ethan rubbed his forehead, feeling as if the weight of the world was on him. "I want to thank each and every one of you for taking a whole day of your time and helping to look for Benjamin. I can't thank you enough. Sarah and I deeply appreciate it and I hope that I can return the favor in a less dire circumstance someday," he said.

∞

Abby was helping Sarah prepare supper when Ethan walked into the cabin. He had dreaded this moment all the way home and it took all of his willpower to look Sarah in the eyes and shake his head. "Nothing," he said. "They seem to have vanished from this world."

"What are we going to do, Ethan?" Sarah said as she wiped her hands on a dishtowel and walked to him.

"The bank is going to loan us the money. We will pay them. Better broke than lose Benjamin," Ethan said as he gave Sarah a hug.

Abigail waited to make sure that they had finished their conversation before speaking. "That settles it. I'm leaving in the morning to find Gideon," she said.

Ethan released Sarah, turning towards Abigail. "Even if you find him, there is nothing he can do. We covered a lot of territory today and did not find a single thing and it's too dangerous for a lady to be riding that far by herself," he said.

"Ethan Oakes, the last time I checked, I was not married to you. I'll ride wherever I want," Abby said trying to sound good-natured, but making her point. "We don't know what will happen before Saturday comes around and Gideon is the only one that is young enough with the experience to handle outlaws. Besides, he owes you that much. It's the least he can do to make up for disappearing for eighteen years."

"You may have a point that it would be good to have him around and I don't think Sarah or I should leave. Why don't you have Marcus do it?" Ethan said.

"Because I don't think he would make much of an effort. He is not exactly Gideon's biggest admirer," Abby said. "I need to get home and fix my own meal. I'm headed out in the morning if I don't get arrested for killing my husband."

"Abigail, I don't want you to bring problems to your marriage for us. This is not your problem," Ethan said.

Abby waved her hand through the air. "I was trying to make light. He will get over it. And it is our problem. We are a community that looks out for its own. Now goodbye," Abby said as she placed kisses on the cheeks of Ethan and Sarah.

Chapter 21

Abigail waited until after supper was over and Winnie had gone outside to do her chores before talking to Marcus. Winnie was beside herself with worry over Benjamin and Abby did not want to upset her further. Her daughter had gone so far as to promise never to hit Benjamin again if he would come home.

"It doesn't look good for finding Benjamin before the ransom is due, does it?" Abby asked.

"No, he is not going to be found. I think they must have ridden all day with him when they took him. He is nowhere near here," Marcus said.

Abby looked at her husband, deciding not to beat around the bush. "I'm going to go find Gideon," she said.

"What? I don't think so," Marcus said.

"Marcus, Ethan needs him," she said.

Marcus stood up from the dinner table. "Is it Ethan or you that needs him?" he said.

"You can go to hell, Marcus Hanson. This is not about me. This is going to end badly if somebody is not here at least to try to do something. I hate to say this, but this kidnapping is too well planned for them to be careless enough to leave a witness," Abby said.

"What makes you think Gideon can do anything that the rest of us cannot?" Marcus said.

"Good God, Marcus. Sheriff Fuller can barely mount a horse anymore and the rest of you are ranchers and farmers. Somebody that knows how to fight is needed and Gideon is the only one that I know and that I would trust," she said.

"A woman cannot just go ride off into the country by herself. If you are hell-bent on this, I will go," Marcus said.

"I can take care of myself and I am a better rider than you. Always have been. You would go make a half-hearted attempt at finding him and then turn around. I will find him," Abby said.

Marcus stared at his wife, his feelings badly hurt. He had tried the whole time that they had been married to be the man that she wanted, but he knew that he always came up short compared to Gideon. Not able to think of anything to say to defend himself, he knew he was defeated and grabbed his hat and walked outdoors.

Abby went to their bedroom and pulled her riding britches out of the drawer where they had been since she had learned that she was pregnant with Winnie. She had given in to Marcus at that time, tired of hearing his preaching about the evils of women wearing pants. Trying on the britches, she could not help but smile when they still fit.

∞

In the morning, Abby explained to Winnie that she was going to be gone for a few days to go get help for Benjamin. Her daughter seemed to take it all in stride except for concern over what she and her daddy were going to eat. Abby assured her that her father could cook when he wanted to but preferred that the woman do it.

Marcus always kept hardtack and jerky for times that he was gone all day and Abby stuffed some of it into her saddlebags and filled her canteen. In the barn she pulled her favorite horse from his stall, a gelding they called Snuggles for his habit of rubbing his head against people. The horse had a soft mouth, allowing her the use of the snaffle bit that she favored. As she was cinching him, she looked at the saddle and thought about how long it had been since she had spent a full day with her butt in one. She tied on her saddlebags and stuck the Winchester rifle into the scabbard. It had been so long since she had shot a gun that she doubted she could hit anything with it, but maybe could come close enough to scare the hell out of somebody if she had to try.

Marcus was waiting outside the barn for her. "When do you think you'll be back?" he asked.

"I don't really know. As quickly as possible. I'll be back by Saturday morning, one way or the other," she said.

"Well, be careful," he said.

She looked at him, thinking that there were times when she would have liked to knock his head off and not even sure why he had just irritated her. If the tables were turned, she imagined she would not be happy with him chasing down his old flame, but she would have made a stand about it and not just sulked. Fight for what you want or get out of the way she thought. "Oh, I will be, don't you worry," she said as she touched her heels into the horse's ribs and took off. Once she got to the road that led to Silverton, she put Snuggles into a trot, his smoothest gait; the faster she found Gideon the better.

∞

Gideon had left Silverton the morning before, headed back to Cimarron. Though he had enjoyed the day of relaxing, he was glad to put it behind him. The town was too wild of a place for him. His plan was to retrace the trail that had led him here and to loop around Last Stand when he got there. Last Stand had occupied his mind a lot since leaving, sometimes thinking that he would return someday, others times not. Either way, he was glad to have had the chance to go home. No matter where he hung his hat, he now knew that a part of him would always belong to Last Stand.

He rode all day, altering his pace between a walk and trot, occasionally putting Buck into a lope. The day was a nice one, a little cooler than usual, making for easy travel for his horse. The sun was starting to get low in the sky and he was getting hungry, ready to find a place to camp for the night. He and the horse had traveled enough for one day.

When he topped a hill, he could see a rider off in the distance headed his way. The sight did not please him. He would have to pass the rider and continue far enough to make sure that he did not end up with a guest for the night since he considered camping with strangers a good way to get your throat slit.

The rider put their horse into a lope when they saw him, making him uneasy enough that out of habit he worked his pistol in its holster a couple of times. As the rider got closer, he recognized something familiar with the way they rode. The person was small and on a big horse. It harkened him back to something long ago that he could not quite recall and then it hit him that it was Abby.

Kicking Buck into a gallop, his mind raced trying to figure out what she was doing a day's ride from her home. He wondered if she had run off to find him, leaving her husband and child in hopes of a life with him. As wrong as that would be, he found himself wishing that it were true.

"Good God, what are you doing out here, Abby?" he said as they pulled their horses up hard.

"It's terrible, Gideon. Somebody kidnapped Benjamin the day before yesterday. The sheriff and everybody else could not even find a track and I decided to go get you. I have a bad feeling on how this is going to turn out if you can't do something," she said.

Gideon felt as if he were gut punched. His legs went limp and he had to rest his hands on the saddle horn so that Abby would not see them tremble. Poor little Benjamin might already be dead or stuck out somewhere scared to death. It didn't seem possible that another little boy that he had crossed paths with might die needlessly through no fault of the child's own doings. Guilt crept in as he wondered if the kidnapping was somehow even tied to his return to Last Stand. Fumbling for words, he said, "This can't be happening."

"I know. I know. What kind of person kidnaps a little boy? And it seems to be very well planned. That is the part that worries me," Abby said.

"I wonder why they targeted Benjamin. Did they leave a note?" Gideon asked.

"They want five thousand dollars on Saturday. I think it has something to do with Ethan's plan to buy the Holden place," Abby said.

"These damn ranchers and their love of land. I've been part of that before, but it never got to the point of harming children. Do you think it might be Frank?" Gideon said.

"I don't know. I can't imagine Frank even stooping to this. He has an awfully lot to lose if he gets caught," Abby said.

"Well, the horses are spent for the day. We might as well camp for the night and get a good start in the morning. You just passed a spot that I camped at on the way to Silverton. It has water and good grass for the horses," Gideon said as he put Buck into a walk.

"I'm going to be so sore. I hope that I can mount my horse in the morning," Abby said.

Gideon laughed. "I can always shove you up there. Why didn't you send Marcus? I can't imagine that he is too thrilled with you right now," Gideon said as they rode side by side down the road.

"Oh, he's not, believe me. I knew he would ride half a day before turning around to head home. Ethan needs you," she said.

"I hope I can do something. If they could not even track them, I'm not sure what I am going to do," Gideon said.

"At least you will be there if you are needed and I fear one way or the other, Ethan is going to need you," Abby said.

They rode on in silence before reaching the spot where Gideon had camped previously. A trail led from the road to a stream fifty yards away. The spot was grassy with large cottonwoods shading the ground and plenty of downed branches for a fire.

"If you think you can get a fire going, I'm going to see if I can find a rabbit or something. Hardtack and jerky get old pretty quick," Gideon said as he started to unsaddle the horses.

"I can still build a fire, Gideon Johann. I didn't spend the last eighteen years twiddling my thumbs, you know?" Abby said and smirked at him.

Gideon saluted her. "Yes, ma'am. I can feel the heat already. Maybe you can also rig up a spit with all that talent."

Pulling his rifle out of the scabbard, he started walking upstream looking for game. Hunting gave him a good excuse to get away from Abby to sort out things. Thinking about Benjamin almost made him nauseas with worry. He would do anything to rescue the boy if there was an opportunity, but having an opportunity was the part he feared would not be provided. Some of the local ranchers were capable of starting a range war, but he had a hard time believing that they would go after a rancher's child. Back in his days as a deputy, he had heard stories of gangs of kidnappers out east that moved about, making him wonder if they had headed west. The only thing that he was sure of was that God help whoever did it if he found them.

There was also Abby showing up out in the middle of nowhere to consider. He was embarrassed for his initial reaction of thinking she had left Marcus for him. It had been a silly fantasy considering the way that their two encounters had gone, but just the same, he knew that she got upset with him because she still cared. He was going to do his best to keep the conversations away from anything that might rile her. Even under such trying circumstance, he looked forward to spending time with her and hoped it could lead to them being friends.

He spied a rabbit making its way to the stream. It must have caught wind of him as it stopped and raised its nose in the air. He aimed at the head and fired, dropping the rabbit. The rifle was overkill and he hoped that he had been on the mark or cleaning it was going to be a mess. He walked over and picked up the game, saw that his shot was true, and cleaned the rabbit there using a knife that he bought at Silverton to replace the one he had left for Benjamin.

When Gideon walked back into camp, Abby had a good fire going and the spit in place. "I could just about eat that rabbit raw. I guess all this riding and fresh air has given me an appetite," she said.

"It won't take long with such a wonderful fire," Gideon said mockingly as he grabbed the spit stick and whittled a point onto it before running it through the rabbit.

The last of the daylight was fading as they sat by the fire and watched the rabbit cook. The conversation lagged as the rabbit sizzled and the aroma of the cooking meat grew stronger. Abby went to her saddle and pulled out a jacket as the temperature started dropping. As she came back to the fire, she checked the meat and pronounced it cooked.

"Tell me about Winnie," Gideon said as he took his first bite of rabbit.

"Winnie," Abby said. "Winnie is just about the best thing that ever happened to me. She is a little spitfire. When I was carrying her, and don't you dare say a word, when I was carrying her, I worried that she would have Marcus's personality, but the moment she was born, I knew better. She came into this world full of fire. She can be a handful and I'm sure that when she gets older that there will be days that I am at my wits end with her, but nobody will ever walk all over her. She is her own person."

"Sounds like her momma to me," Gideon said.

"True, but she is even more determined than I ever thought about being. I don't think that she would ever let herself be railroaded the way I have in the past," she said.

"She must make you very proud," he said.

"So whereabouts have you been all these years?" Abby asked as she blew on the piece of rabbit to cool it.

"You name it and I probably have been there," Gideon said. "I've been up in the Wyoming and Montana Territories, here in Colorado, and down in New Mexico. Been to Texas too, but that place is too damn hot for my likings. I've worked as a deputy and ranch hand mainly. I also did some work as a hired gun. Got involved in the Colfax County War on the side of the settlers, but I quit that when innocent people started getting killed. I've seen a lot of this country. It's a beautiful place when people don't make a mess of it."

Gideon pulled a leg off the rabbit and handed it to Abby. "Are your parents still alive and how are your brother Tom and your sisters?" he asked

"Momma and Daddy are doing well. They still live in the old home place and Tom runs things now. He and his wife built a house down the road from them. Daddy still helps Tom and Marcus when things get busy. Sissy is married and in Denver and Rose moved back east to Baltimore. Don't ask me why," Abby said.

"I cleaned up my mother's gravesite. It had grown up after Frank ran Ethan out of there a few years back. I never imagined it going unattended and a mess. I don't know how I thought it would stay maintained," Gideon said.

"Your parents were good people. I still think about them sometimes and miss them," she said.

"Yes, they were but they probably would have thought they failed as parents if they had lived," he said.

Abby finished off the rabbit leg and tossed the bones into the fire. A chill went through her and she pulled her jacket tightly shut. She wanted so badly to know more. "Gideon, if you ever come to a point in your life where you can talk about what happened, I would love to know. You could write me a letter or something. I spent so many years wondering about you," she said.

He stood and started pacing as soon as she spoke. He could feel the words wanting to start to bubble up again just as they did with Mary and at the grave. Being back in Last Stand had opened a wound that he had sealed off for so long. If anybody deserved to know, he knew that person was Abby, and he did not have the will to hold onto it any longer. "There were four of us that got separated from the unit in a skirmish and we were trying to make our way back. There was a sound of something running through the brush and I thought we were being attacked. So much of what we dealt with was guerrilla type fighting. They would come at you from out of nowhere. I fired at the sound and it was a little boy about the same age as Benjamin. I hit him in the chest and I had to watch him die. There was so much fear showing in his eyes as he gasped for breath. I held his hand and told him I was sorry. He lived maybe five minutes and then we had to leave him. His family may have never have found him for all I know. I've seen those eyes looking up at me thousands of times ever since."

Abby watched him pace the whole time he was talking. When he finished, she closed her eyes and covered her mouth with her hand, trying to imagine what Gideon had been living with for so long. In all the years since he had disappeared, she had imagined a thousand different scenarios of what had happened and none of them had been nearly as bad as the actual truth. "Oh, Gideon, that is the saddest thing I have ever heard. I understand your feeling guilty, but that is what happens in war. Innocent people are killed all the time. They always do. Ruining your life is not going to bring him back, nor is it going to atone for your mistake. Being happy and a charitable person will bring far more honor to that little boy than the path you have chosen," she said.

He sat back down and started to cry. There was no way that he could stop it and it embarrassed him terribly. After so many of years of carrying the burden of the secret, he marveled that it was gone in a few words. He did not know if it would last, but right now, he felt so much relief that he was physically weak.

Abby came over and sat beside him, resting her head on his shoulder as he cried. She did not say anything, just waited for him to cry out the years of pain. When he stopped, she did not move and neither of them spoke. Finally, after minutes had passed, she was ready to talk. "Gideon, I have a secret to tell you too. I know now it not the best time, but it is probably the only time we will ever have," she said as he uncovered his face and looked at her. His face looked so pathetic that she wanted to hold him and make the hurt go away as she did when Winnie skinned a knee. She had no idea how he would react to her news, but she was sure that now was the time to get everything out in the open. "Oh, I don't know where to begin with this. I guess just come out and say it. Please just let me get it all out there before you say anything. Gideon, this is going to be such a shock, but you have a daughter. When I found out I was carrying your child, I told Momma and Daddy, and of course, they were horrified. You know how religious they are and they were so ashamed. They would not let me write you and they said they would disown me if I did. I was so young and scared. That is what I meant when I said Winnie would not be railroaded as I was. They were more worried about somebody finding out than doing what was right. I know I should have written you and you would have married me, but they had me so scared. I just caved in. I don't know if you remember, but my momma had a younger sister in Wyoming, Aunt Rita, that could not have children. I went up there and had Joann and they raised her as their own. I named her Joann after Johann. Nobody in Last Stand was any the wiser. Of course, everybody up there knew the truth and Joann found out. She knows I am her real mother and she knows about you. We are very close. She visits some summers and she is seventeen now. Winnie thinks she is about the greatest thing on earth and she has your blue eyes. When she is here, I'm afraid people will figure it out because they are so blue like yours. Marcus would die if he knew she was ours. I know all of this must be hard to believe, but you would be proud of her if you met her. She is smart and beautiful and has a kind heart. I don't know what else to say."

Gideon kept looking at her, his mind trying to take in what Abby had said. He was already so shaken from his confession that the news was hard to comprehend. It felt as if he were eavesdropping on somebody else's conversation. "I have a daughter," he repeated numbly as he stood up and started pacing again. "You and I had a baby together?"

"Yes, Gideon, we did," she said.

He stopped walking and allowed everything that had just transpired to soak in - Abby knew his secret and he had a daughter. It was time to gain control of himself he decided. He took a deep breath and exhaled slowly. Staying calm and alert had kept him alive through many close calls, and he willed it in himself now. Glancing over at Abby, she was looking overwhelmed herself and made him wonder if two secrets had ever changed lives as much as theirs had. He was in control of himself now, just physically drained. "Abby, I wish that you would have written me. I understand why you didn't and God knows I'm the last person on earth that would have the right to fault you for it. Quite a night, huh? You learn my long held secret and I find out I have a daughter. That feels so strange to say. I have a daughter. Tomorrow I may be more miserable than I have ever been in my life, but tonight I feel such a relief to have it all out in the open. Tell me about Joann."

Abby started to cry now. She was not sure why, she guessed she was like Gideon, relieved to have the secrets out in the open. Wiping her eyes with the back of her hands, she smiled. "She is pretty if I do say so myself. Tall, and lanky like you, and those blue eyes. Her mouth and eyes are shaped like mine. She is kind and thoughtful. Aunt Rita and Uncle Jake did a good job raising her and they have been so good about letting me be part of her life. It would have killed me if they hadn't. She has asked me a thousand questions about you," she said.

He sat down beside her and patted her leg. "I have a hard time believing I'm a father," he said. "I never thought I would be one of those."

"Now you know why I got so upset when you made a joke about it like it was some roll in the hay," she said.

Gideon giggled like a child and rubbed his scar. "I guess so," he said.

"I wish you could see her picture. I have one at home," Abby said.

Gideon got up and walked over to his saddlebags to pull out the bottle of whiskey. "Let's have a sip in honor of the end of secrets," he said as he uncorked the bottle and handed it to Abby.

Abby held up the bottle. "To the end of secrets," she said and took a drink before handing it back to Gideon.

Gideon took a sip and then returned the bottle to the saddlebags. "We better get some sleep. Tomorrow's going to be a long day. I'm going to find Benjamin," he said with a renewed determination that somehow he would succeed.

He added wood to the fire and made his bed on the opposite side of it from Abby's spot. As soon as they bedded down, Abby knew what she was going to do even before she admitted it to herself. Cheating on Marcus may have been a sin, but as far as she was concerned, she and Gideon had already paid for all the sins that they would ever commit. Missing the one opportunity that she would ever have to spend the night with the only man that she had ever loved would be the real sin, and life was too hard not to take the love when it was there. "Gideon, come keep me warm," she said.

He walked slowly over to her. She was on her side with her back to him and he slid under the blanket, nuzzling up against her and catching a whiff of the scent of her perfume still lingering on her neck. The fragrance was the same that she had worn as a girl and the nostalgia it caused was so overpowering that it sent him reeling back to those days. He could not help himself but to kiss the back of her neck.

She rolled onto her back and looked into his eyes. "Love me, Gideon," she said.

Chapter 22

Gideon gently shook Abby. "Wake up, sleepyhead. We have to ride and get home. Benjamin needs us," he said.

Abby slowly opened her eyes, smiling at Gideon. She leaned in and kissed him on the lips. "So last night wasn't a dream after all," she said.

He smiled at her and brushed the hair out of her face. "Well, if that was a dream, it was the best one that I ever had," he said.

"There's that smile. You should wear it more often. It looks good on you," Abby said.

"Okay, let's eat and get going," Gideon said as he got up and started pulling hardtack and jerky out of his saddlebags.

Abby stood up and started walking stiffly, grabbing the canteens to fill at the stream. "I'm not sure which is sorer, the side that rode the horse all day or the side that you rode all night," she said.

"Abby," Gideon said, embarrassed by her comment.

She burst out giggling. "Let me enjoy our one day together."

"So I guess having a daughter is not a dream either. Do you think she hates me?" he said.

"No. No. No. She understands that you did not know about her. She is just curious, as you would expect," Abby said.

"You didn't let her know I was back then?" Gideon asked.

"As badly as our first couple of meetings went, I was not about to let her in on it until you were gone. I just didn't see any way that something good could come from it," she said.

"I suppose not," he said.

"I haven't ridden this much in years. It's a long ways back," Abby said.

"We can tell everybody we met up this morning. Maybe it will give you some cover with Marcus," Gideon said.

The remark brought her back to the reality of the situation. "Yeah, we probably should say that. You know, Gideon, one bullet and one letter not sent changed the whole course of our lives."

"I know. There's no point on dwelling on it now. Let's just enjoy the day as much as possible considering all that's going on back home," he said.

∞

Benjamin had barely eaten anything since the kidnapping. He had never recovered from the trauma of Marcus almost discovering them and still believed that it had been his pa, worrying continuously that Ethan would come back to be murdered. The couple of times that he had tried eating, he immediately threw it up, infuriating Jasper.

"Goddamn kid, it's bad enough being stuck in this cave without having to smell puke," Jasper said.

"Leave the kid alone. You'd be scared to if it was you," Walter said.

"Sitting around all day with that little baby is getting on my nerves. I never knew that time could go so slow. Hell, scooping cow shit is better than this," Jasper said.

Walter put his hand on Benjamin's shoulder. "You only got two more days in here and then you will get to go home. Just hang in there," he said.

"Is anybody going to get killed?" Benjamin asked.

"No, nobody is going to get killed. They won't come back to this cave now that they already checked it. Your pa will pay the money and then you will go home," Walter said.

"My pa don't have any money," Benjamin said.

"The bank will loan him money to get you back. Don't worry, he will pay to get you home," Walter said.

Jasper was pacing in his agitated state. "Will everybody just shut the hell up? All this talking gets on my nerves. If your daddy don't get the money we will slit your throat," he said.

Benjamin started to cry and Jasper moved towards him with his arm drawn to backhand him, but Walter stepped between them to intervene. "Sit down. You are not going to touch him," he said.

Jasper stopped and looked up at Walter. He knew that on his best day that he would never win a fight with him. Walter was too big and he had seen him fight. The man knew how to hold his own in a brawl. "Okay, okay Walter. I'm just a little worked up. I didn't mean nothing," he said and sat on the cave floor.

"Nothing is going to happen to you Benjamin. Your pa will get the money and you'll be home for supper Saturday," Walter said.

∞

Ethan feared that by the time that Saturday came around that Sarah was going to have a breakdown. She wasn't sleeping or eating and she could barely carry on a conversation with him. Her mind seemed to be in a fog and conversation barely registered with her. He wished now that Abby had stayed around. Sarah needed a woman to talk to and he held out little hope that she would find

Gideon. He had no expectations that Gideon could accomplish anything that they had not already done to try to find Benjamin anyway.

"Sarah, let me fix you something to eat and then we can take a nap. We both need some rest," Ethan said.

"Do you think Benjamin is still alive?" she asked, ignoring what he had said.

"Yes, Sarah, I know he is alive. I can feel it. God would not take our boy from us," he said.

"Why would God let them take him then, Ethan?" Sarah asked as she sat down at the table and started bouncing her fingers on it as if she were playing the piano.

"Sarah, there has been evil since the beginning of time. It doesn't mean that it will triumph. Please have some faith. It's all that we have right now," Ethan said.

"I don't want to live without my baby. I'd just shrivel up and die anyway if he is gone," she said.

Ethan walked over to her. "Give me hug. I need one," he said. She stood up with her arms to her side as he hugged her. "I promise you that we are going to get Benjamin back."

∞

Gideon and Abby were getting close to home. They had made good time in their traveling and had a little over an hour of sunlight left before dusk. Most of the day had been spent reminiscing about the old times and avoiding subjects that neither one of them were ready to discuss.

"Do you think I will ever be able to see Joann?" Gideon finally asked.

"I hope so. I know Joann would want to and I think Aunt Rita and Uncle Jake would be okay with it. They know that they are always going to be in her life. She usually comes every other summer and was here last year. Maybe she could come again this year. Do you think you are going to stick around now?" Abby said.

"I don't know. It's too soon to tell. I don't really know if anything has changed or not. When this is all over, I might feel the need to start running again. I just don't know. I feel better than I have in years, but who's to say if it will last. How things turn out with Benjamin might make a difference too," Gideon said.

"So, if you don't stay, you'd ride to Wyoming?" she asked.

"Yeah, maybe. I don't know what I would say to her. I'd just like to lay eyes on her. Do you think it would be good for her?" he said.

"I think so. She understands that it's not as if you ran out on her and now want to be part of her life. She knows that you didn't know and she is curious. I don't think any harm would come from it," Abby said.

"Abby, what would you do if I decided to stay?" Gideon asked.

"What do you mean?" she asked.

"I don't know. How do you think it would affect you?" he said.

"Gideon, I'm not sure what you are asking, but if it is what I think it is, I don't know. I have another daughter to think about and everything else. Is that what you are asking?" Abby said.

"Maybe, I don't know either," Gideon said as they reached the crossroads where they would go their separate ways.

"Gideon, in case this is our last time ever alone together, I want you to know I love you. I loved you when I was sixteen and I love you now. And I have no regrets about last night. We both deserved it. Life is too short not to take the happiness when it is offered," she said.

Gideon closed his eyes and rubbed them. He was about to say words he never thought he would ever say again. "Abby, I love you too. No matter what happens from here on out, it has all been worth it. And even though it never happened the way we wished it had, I'm glad we had Joann together," he said.

Abby leaned over and wrapped her hands around Gideon's neck, pulling him to her. She kissed him hard on the mouth and then turned her horse and rode away without looking back.

He watched her ride off until she was out of sight, wondering about the strange twists that life takes. His life had changed more in the last few weeks than it had in the previous ten years and it would have been too much to handle if not for the fact that the changes were good. Whether he ever saw Abby again or got to meet Joann, there was no going back. He was ready to admit that he did not loath himself any longer. The place that he had avoided all these years had held the key. He had found redemption at Last Stand. Now he needed to find Benjamin to make it complete. He put Buck into a lope towards Ethan's place.

Ethan heard Chase barking on the porch and walked out with his rifle. The dog was turning out to be good at alerting to visitors and as Ethan saw Gideon coming, a sense of relief settled over him. Whether Gideon could help or not, he would be there for him and Sarah. "I see she found you," he said as Gideon rode up into the yard.

"She did. Any word?" Gideon said as he climbed down from the horse.

"Nothing. I got the money arranged. There's nothing to do, but wait for Saturday," Ethan said.

Gideon walked onto the porch. His friend looked bad, dark under the eyes and his face puffy from lack of sleep.

Stress was etched onto his forehead and around the eyes. "So you could not track them at all?" he asked.

"They grabbed him in that rocky spot between here and the schoolhouse. You could ride an army through there and nobody would know it. We had twenty men looking all day Tuesday and found nothing. I think they took him a day's ride from here," Ethan said.

"So the sheriff has no idea about who did it then?" Gideon said.

Ethan shook his head as he sat down on the porch and started petting Chase.

"How is Sarah holding up?" Gideon asked as he sat down beside Ethan and patted his friend's leg.

"Not good. If we lose him, I think she will lose her mind," Ethan said.

"We're not going to lose him. I'm going to see if sheriff will deputize me in the morning. Where are you supposed to leave the money?" Gideon said.

"At Sand Creek Bridge," Ethan said.

"That's a strange choice. Not a good place from which to escape," Gideon said.

"That's what I thought. I think they have something up their sleeve. This was too well planned for a choice like that," Ethan said.

"You're probably right," Gideon said.

"So you and Abby didn't kill each on the road, I take it?" Ethan asked.

"No, that is the one good thing that came from this. We met up this morning and had all day to talk. I think we came to an understanding," Gideon said.

Ethan noticed that Gideon did not make eye contact when he spoke and Gideon always made eye contact. His friend was lying to him and he was sure that the reason why was because they had spent the night together. He knew it as sure as his name was Ethan Oakes. The preacher in him might not approve, but the part of him that was a friend was glad. As much as those two had suffered, if it brought them some happiness and closure, he was all for it. "Well, that's good," he said.

"Let's go in and I can see Sarah. Maybe reassure her," Gideon said to change the subject.

"Gideon, I'm glad you're back, but there's nothing that you can do. We are going to pay the money and hope that they keep their end of the bargain. That's the only thing we can do," Ethan said.

Gideon looked at Ethan, trying to find words to convince him that he would get their son back. He was at a loss on how he would do it. Sometimes during the war, he had had to will himself to live. It had saved him more than once when he should have died. He would will himself to rescue Benjamin now. Putting his arm around Ethan's shoulders, they walked towards the door of the cabin.

∞

Sligo started riding to the cave at sunset. To be cautious, he stayed off the main trails all the way there. Frank's insistence that he go check on Walter and Jasper had put him in an ill mood. In his mind, the two ranch hands should be capable of spending a week in the cave without him having to babysit them, but he brought some extra supplies just in case they were running low.

Darkness had settled in by the time that he reached the mouth of the cave. As he was getting off his horse, Jasper came out of the cave leading their two horses. "Jasper, it's Sligo," he whispered.

Jasper let out a holler. "Damn, Sligo, you liked to have scared the piss out of me," he said.

"Quit being such a girl, Jasper. I just came by to check on you guys and leave some supplies. How is everything going?" Sligo asked.

"It gets old taking these horses out every night to feed and go getting them before light. It's a half a mile walk to grass. Did you bring us some whiskey?" Jasper said.

"I wanted to bring you a bottle, but Frank said you don't need no whiskey. How is the boy doing?" Sligo asked.

"I guess okay. He's a little baby. Cries sometimes and ain't eating much," Jasper said.

"I'd talk if I was you and the way you hollered when I called out to you," Sligo said.

"Get off my ass, Sligo. This ain't no fun," Jasper said.

Sligo handed Jasper the sack of supplies. "Think how rich you are going to be when this is through. Keep that in mind and take care of that boy. You mistreat him and you will answer to me. Understand?" Sligo said.

"Don't worry. I'm not stupid," Jasper said.

Sligo mounted his horse. "See you Saturday morning," he said.

Chapter 23

Frank decided to go to town on Friday morning. It was time for a haircut and he wanted to visit the bank to question Druthers. He also planned to find out if the sheriff had any tricks up his sleeve for the ransom exchange. Pulling one of his white shirts out of the wardrobe, he viewed himself in the mirror as he buttoned it. It would be hot, but he decided he would wear his black jacket. It would be preferable to be a little warm in order to carry the magnitude he craved. He pulled a couple of cigars from his humidor and put them in his pocket. His wardrobe was complete with the addition of his new hat.

Once in town, Frank's first stop was at the bank, walking into Mr. Druthers office unannounced and sitting down without invitation. He pulled out a cigar, biting off the cap and spitting it on the floor, before lighting the stogie.

Mr. Druthers, trying to ignore the rude behavior of his biggest depositor, forced a smile. "What can I do for you today, Mr. DeVille?" he said.

"I was wanting to know if Ethan Oakes got the money for the ransom," Frank said.

"Mr. DeVille, my other customer's business is confidential," Mr. Druthers said.

Frank took a draw on his cigar and let out a huge plume of smoke. "Listen you little weasel, you're lucky that the money you gave my wife to run off with, I did not take out of your hide. Now answer me," he said.

Ignoring the question, the banker chose to defend himself. "That was a joint account. She was perfectly within her rights to withdraw that money. I had no recourse but to let her have it," he said.

"You could have stalled her and got word to me and you know it. If you would have, I could have stopped the bitch from leaving and saved me the humiliation. The reason I want to know if Ethan has the money is that I don't want his son killed over a tight ass banker refusing to loan it to him. I will guarantee the loan if necessary. Now answer the Goddamn question or I am going to turn Sligo loose on you," Frank said.

The banker pursued what little lips he had and ran his hand across his bald head. "Mr. Oakes will have his money. It is all arranged," he said.

"Now, wouldn't it have been easier to answer me the first time and save us both the irritation," Frank said as he stood and tapped ash off the cigar onto the floor. "Good day, Mr. Druthers."

Frank walked out of the bank, headed towards the sheriff's office. As he looked down the street, he almost bit his cigar in two. He saw Gideon tying his horse up in front of the office and going inside. Muttering to himself, Frank said, "I'll be Goddamn. Where in the hell did he come from?" he said to no one. "I guess I'll get my haircut and then find out what the hell is going on."

Sheriff Fuller was sitting at his desk, sipping coffee, when Gideon walked in. "Well, look what the cat drug in. I didn't think I would be seeing you so soon," the sheriff said.

"I got word on what happened and I came back to help. I was hoping that you would deputize me in case there's trouble," Gideon said and sat down in a chair facing the sheriff.

The sheriff sat his cup down and slapped the desk. "It's the damndest thing I've ever seen, Gideon. You know, I'm a pretty fair tracker and there was nothing, not even a horse turd. I'm at a loss," he said.

"It looks as if they knew what they were doing. I've heard of kidnapping rings back east. I wonder if they've moved west?" Gideon said.

"I don't know. I go back and forth between thinking it was outsiders and somebody that knows this place pretty good," Sheriff Fuller said.

"There has to be more than one of them. Has any strangers been to town?" Gideon asked.

"Not a soul. The saloons and stores are keeping their eyes open for me. Now why are you wanting me to make you a deputy?" the sheriff asked.

"Because we don't know what is going to happen tomorrow and I don't want to be accused of being a vigilante. I'm not going to do anything to endanger Benjamin, but I'll be ready if needed. If they hurt him, I will hunt them to hell and back and I just as soon be on the side of the law when I did it," Gideon said.

"Fair enough. You know that they're holding all the cards. We are going to have to sit back and see what happens unless we want to get Benjamin killed," Sheriff Fuller said.

"I know. Do you think scouting around today would do any good?" Gideon asked.

"Gideon, I don't think they are around here. Whichever direction they went, they kept going for a long time. I know I'm too old to go chasing them down. If I were you, I would just be ready to ride tomorrow after it's over. I suspect you would be better off going it alone," he said.

"I don't like being at their mercy to do what they see fit with Benjamin," Gideon said.

"Me neither. I just don't see no choice. Now stand up and raise your right hand," the sheriff said and waited for Gideon to get to his feet. "Do you swear to uphold the laws of the State of Colorado to protect and serve the citizens to the best of your ability?"

"I do," Gideon said.

"I'm not sure if I got that all right, but it's close enough," he said and handed Gideon a badge out of his desk drawer.

Gideon smiled. "Close enough for swearing in a drifter anyway," he said as he pinned the badge on his shirt.

"I'll see you here in the morning then," the sheriff said.

Gideon walked out into the street thinking about going to the saloon before deciding better of it. Life was complicated enough already without seeing Mary. He chuckled to himself at the thought that sleeping with Mary would now feel like cheating on somebody else's wife.

Frank was walking towards the sheriff's office and saw Gideon come out the door. He had hoped he would be gone by now and cursed under his breath when he saw the sun reflecting off the badge. Deciding that talking to him would be the best thing, he kept walking.

"Gideon, you are back," Frank said.

"Yeah, it's getting to be a habit I guess. I got word about Benjamin," Gideon said.

"It's a terrible thing. I know you don't care for my man Sligo, but I had him help with trying to find the boy. It's as if he disappeared. I see the sheriff made you a deputy. If there is anything we can do, you let us know. Me and you have never seen eye to eye, but we have to bury our differences for things like this," Frank said.

"I don't think there is much to do. Pay the ransom and hope it all comes out okay," Gideon said. "I have to get going now."

"You take care," Frank said.

Frank watched as Gideon rode away without even bothering to say goodbye. He would make the arrogant bastard pay for returning to Last Stand. Gideon never knew when to leave well enough alone and he would teach him this time. Climbing on his horse, he headed home to talk to Sligo.

He found Sligo in the barn brushing down his horse. "Come on to the house. We need to talk," he said before unsaddling his horse and putting it in a stall.

As they walked to the house, Frank said, "Gideon is back and the sheriff deputized him. I'm going to make the bastard regret it."

Frank went into his office and shut the door behind Sligo. Sitting down at his desk, he pulled two cigars from the humidor and for the first time ever, offered one to Hank. He waited to talk until both cigars were lit and burning well. "Okay, here is the plan," he began. "Tonight after dark, you are going to take a note to the bridge and make sure to put it where they will see it. It will tell them to take the money and leave it at the base of that big rock at Sulfur Pond. It will then tell them to come back to the rock an hour after delivering the money to get the note to tell them where the kid is and if anything funny goes on, a gun will be fired and that will be the signal to kill the kid. What do you think so far?" he said.

"Sounds like you got it all figured out. What's the rest of it?" Sligo asked.

Frank took a big puff on his cigar and then started waving it through the air for emphasis as he talked. "You ride over to the cave in the morning and send Walter with the note to leave when he picks up the money. I was going to have you watch him in case there was trouble, but I don't think there will be. You stay with Jasper. Just tell them we're going to leave the kid there. When Walter gets back, kill them and lay them out with their guns in their hands like they shot each other. Make sure you don't forget to shoot their guns as many times as you have to shoot them and put five gold pieces in each of their pockets. Then I want you to slit the kid's throat. It will be safer that way and I want to make Ethan and Gideon pay for returning and sticking his nose into it. I've put up with one or the other of them my whole life and now it is payback time. You should have plenty of time to ride out the back way. Just be as careful as you were the first time about tracks. When you get a half of a mile away or so, head for the road. You won't have to worry about tracks then," Frank said.

Hank was starting to feel sick. He never envisioned killing the kid and the thought of walking up to him to slit his throat made him want to puke. He had done a lot of despicable things in his life, but he had never sunk to killing children. "You sure you want me to kill the kid, Boss?" he asked.

"What's the matter? Aren't you man enough to do it? You're always running your mouth about how big and bad you are. Surely you can take care of a kid," Frank said.

"It's not that, but if we kill the kid and get caught, it goes from prison to hanging," Hank said.

"How are we going to get caught? I've thought about everything," Frank said.

"Won't they hear all the extra shooting?" Hank asked.

"You should be far enough away that the gun shots won't carry that far, but after you kill them, you can take their guns back in the cave to shoot them. You won't have to go back in there very far to kill most of the sound. Take a little torch with you," Frank said.

"Okay, Boss. I don't hanker to kill a kid, but I guess it's best," Hank said.

"Go into town tonight after you drop off the note. Relax and have some beer and keep your ear to the ground to make sure there's no surprises. I don't think there will be. They want that kid alive. Buy Doc a beer if you get the chance," Frank said as he threw a twenty-dollar gold piece towards Hank and then waved his hand to dismiss him.

∞

Gideon returned to the cabin at noon to find a wagon and team of horses out by the barn. On the porch there was a young girl playing on the swing. Looking her over, he knew it had to be Winnie as her facial feature made her a dead giveaway to be Abby's daughter. Inside the cabin, he found Ethan, Sarah, Abby, and Marcus all sitting at the table. Quickly scanning the group, Marcus's face practically dripped with contempt and Abby was having a hard time making eye contact, but Ethan and Sarah looked as if the company had distracted them enough to relax a little. "Well, if we had some cards, we would have enough for poker," he said.

"Gideon," Marcus said as a greeting.

"Marcus, good to see you," Gideon said.

"I see the sheriff pinned a star on you. What did he have to say?" Ethan asked.

"Not much. After we get Benjamin back, I'm going to try to find them. They won't have time to cover their tracks this time. I'm going to make the drop-off. That way it will be the law that they are dealing with if they try anything," Gideon said.

Sarah stood and walked to Gideon, placing her hands on his chest for emphasis. "Gideon, I don't want you being a hero. I just want Benjamin back. We can always make more money, but we can't make another Benjamin," she said.

Gideon put his hands around Sarah's arms. "Sarah, I promise you, I will do nothing to jeopardize Benjamin. I just want to be the one to do it so that if there is trouble, Ethan will not be in danger. Okay?" he said.

Sarah kissed his cheek. "Okay."

Chapter 24

Jasper was up pacing, more agitated than the day before. The stay in the cave was making him crazy. He had never counted on the isolation being this hard and he couldn't take it any longer. "I got enough money to go buy a bottle of whiskey and I'm going to town to get it. I can't take another minute sitting here waiting," he said.

"It will be over tomorrow. You can hang on for one more day," Walter said.

"It ain't over tomorrow. We'll be running for days to get away. They'll be wanting that money back," Jasper said.

"Come on, Jasper. Just sit tight another day," Walter pleaded.

"They should have packed us some whiskey if they were going to hole us up here. I'll just ride into town, get a bottle, and come back. I'll be back way before night and nobody will think anything of it," Jasper said as he moved towards the back of the cave to retrieve his horse.

"Somebody might see you leave," Walter said in one last attempt to stop Jasper.

"There's a better chance of the Indians coming back for their moccasins than a white man riding around here," Jasper said as he pulled his horse into the front of the cave.

Walter stood idly and watched Jasper saddle his horse. He knew he could stop him if he really wanted, but he just didn't have it in him to fight that day, and besides that, some whiskey would go a long way in soothing the boredom. "Be careful and don't waste time. You know if the boss catches you, he will take your head off," he said.

"The boss can kiss my ass. He hasn't been sitting in a cave all week," Jasper said as he led his horse out of the cave and mounted.

Jasper's ride into town was uneventful, never seeing another person until he was almost to Last Stand. Riding down the main street, he checked and did not see Sligo's horse tied anywhere. His plan was to go into the saloon, buy his bottle, and head back. When he walked in, the first thing that he saw was Mary leaning against the bar, laughing as if she were having the time of her life. He immediately decided that maybe spending some time in a saloon talking to a woman would be a whole lot more enjoyable than drinking in a cave, listening to Walter jabber and smelling his farts.

He sat down at a table and called out for a bottle. Mary brought the whiskey over with two glasses. "Buy me a drink, Jasper?" she asked.

"Why sure, Mary. It would be nice to have your company," Jasper said.

"What are you doing in here on a Friday afternoon?" Mary asked as she filled the glasses.

"Uh, Sligo gave us the afternoon off," he said.

"What's gotten into him? I never knew he did anything nice," she said and took her first sip.

"I guess there is a first time for everything," Jasper said before taking a drink and swishing it in his mouth before swallowing. He closed his eyes and tilted his head up as if he was receiving divine inspiration.

"Have you been working hard?" Mary asked.

"Working cattle for Sligo is always hard. He never lets up," he said.

"I bet so. Have you heard about Benjamin Oakes being kidnapped?" she asked.

Jasper laughed nervously. "I don't know nothing about that kid getting kidnapped," he said.

Mary took a sip of whiskey, watching Jasper. She found his behavior odd in the way that he answered her question. "So you heard about it then. What do you think happened?" she asked.

He laughed again nervously, avoiding eye contact and taking a quick sip of his whiskey. "I tell you, I don't know nothing about that kidnapping," he said with his voice sounding like a child trying to cover up a misdeed.

She was sure he was lying now and slowly took another sip of whiskey trying to think what next to do. "Why don't you take me upstairs, Jasper? You look like you could use a good roll in the hay," she said.

Jasper leaned over close to her. "Mary, I don't got enough money," he said.

"Jasper, it is your lucky day. Not only did you get the afternoon off, but Mr. Vander said that he wanted me to give one of my regular customers a free poke in appreciation of their business and Jasper you are my favorite cowboy in this whole town," Mary said.

"Really, Mary, I'm your favorite?" Jasper asked.

"Shoot, Jasper, I'd have got you to marry me a long time ago except I knew you can't afford a wife," she said and grabbed his hand.

"Well, let's go then," he said, standing up and grabbing his bottle and glass.

Mary led him by the hand into her room and shut the door. Determined to be in control, she did not want to give him time to think and started unbuttoning his shirt with him pinned against the door. Pulling the shirt open, she started kissing his chest. "Jasper, if you ever came into money, we could run off somewhere and get married. Start a new life. Wouldn't that be nice?" she said between kisses.

"Uh-huh," he moaned.

She continued kissing him, working down his belly. "We could have us some real fun if we were married and had money. You like fun don't you Jasper?" Mary said.

"Oh, Mary," Jasper groaned.

She knelt down on her knees, unbuckling his gun belt, his belt, and then the buttons on his breeches. She yanked the trousers down and the musky smell hit her so hard that she had to stop. Trying not to break the mood, she led him waddling with his breeches at his ankles to the washstand. She needed information, but there was no way that she was going to put her mouth on his pecker without scrubbing it first. She soaped him, running her hands up and down his penis. "You are so big and hard. A stud horse doesn't have anything on you. Let me get you good and clean and then I got a surprise for you," she said as she wiped the soap off with a towel.

She put her mouth on him and started working while he moaned like a cat purring. She looked up and his eyes were rolled so far back in his head that she thought they might flip over and come back around. "I could do this for you every day if we were married. Wouldn't you like that, Jasper? If we just had money," Mary said.

"Yes, Mary, yes," Jasper cried out as if he had found religion. "I'm going to be rich tomorrow."

She went back down on him, arousing him as much as she dared. "If you're going to be rich, we can run off and get married. I can't wait to please you every night, Jasper. If you're going to be rich tomorrow, you must be part of the kidnapping. Is that it?" Mary said, mouthing him before he could speak.

"Yes, Mary, I'm part of it," Jasper said rapidly.

"I'll keep pleasuring you and you tell me all about it," she said.

"I can't tell you about it. It's a secret," he said.

Mary paused, waiting for him to need her so badly that he would tell her everything. His face was so contorted that she would have laughed if she could have. "Now Jasper, if we are going to get married, we can't have secrets. You need to tell me all about it so I know what to expect for meeting up with you," she said and waited.

"Okay, okay, don't stop and I'll tell you," Jasper said and then moaned as Mary resumed. "Frank and Hank planned it all. Hank kidnapped him and took him to Moccasin Cave and me and Walter have been keeping him there ever since. Hank is coming in the morning to tell us what to do. I get a thousand dollars and me and Walter will make our getaway and nobody will know Frank and Hank did it."

Mary almost stopped from shock upon hearing that Sligo and DeVille were the ringleaders. She realized that she should have known that Sligo had his hand in it as everything evil around here involved him. "Jasper, you've made me so happy. I can't wait to marry you," she said.

She steeled herself for what was to come and went to work to get it finished. Jasper screamed out like a girl when he came, making her worry that Mr. Vander would be knocking the door down at any second coming to her rescue. Pulling Jasper down onto the bed, she bathed his face in kisses. "Jasper, I love you and I'm going to make you so happy. Do you feel good, Honey?" she cooed to him.

Jasper was so relaxed that he looked as if he might fall asleep. "Uh-huh, I feel real good," he said.

"Where can I meet up with you tomorrow? Where are we headed?" Mary asked.

"Can you ride? Do you even have a horse?" Jasper said.

She smiled and kissed his lips, relieved that he was still thinking about her riding with him. Getting more information out of him was going to be easy. "Baby, I've been riding horses since I could walk. I know horseflesh too. I go down to the stable all the time and see what that old coot has for sale. He's got one that I've had my eye on. I'm going to buy it for our escape. Now where are we going?" she said.

Jasper tucked his hands behind his head, looking as if he thought he was the king of the castle. "We are going to ride the back country to Pagosa Springs and then take the trails north. Walter is from over in there and knows all the trails. We got a lot of riding to do. Depending on how hard they chase us, we may go to Denver or keep going up into the Wyoming Territory," Jasper said.

"So you don't know where you pick up the money or anything? You're not going to hurt the boy are you?" she asked.

"Nah, Sligo hasn't told us anything. I guess they won't hurt him. Nothing's been said about it," he said.

"I'll ride out to Pagosa tomorrow morning and be waiting for you off the road going north out of there. You had better get back to the cave. If Sligo catches you, he might kill you. I love you, Jasper. I am going to make you so happy," Mary said and started kissing him again.

"Do you think I could have a poke before I go?" Jasper asked.

"Honey, you have got to go. I'm going to give you so much loving that you're going to think you have died and gone to heaven," she said before jumping up and topping her glass off with whiskey.

Jasper got up reluctantly, buttoning his breeches and putting his gun belt back on. "I don't know what time we will get to Pagosa Springs. It's hard to say," he said.

Mary gave him a kiss and handed him his bottle. "Don't you worry, I'll be there waiting. Don't you dare get yourself killed now," she said as she led him to the door.

With the door locked behind her, she took a drink of the whiskey, swirling it around in her mouth until the burning had made it completely numb and then spitting it in the washbasin. As she watched out the window, she took a big sip and swallowed slowly, feeling it burn all the way down her throat. She gave Jasper a little wave as he looked up at her window when he mounted his horse.

After Jasper rode out of sight, she peeled off her saloon clothes and put on her best skirt and blouse. The clothes had not been worn in ages and she stopped at the mirror, admiring herself and fixing her hair back in place. She managed to smile at herself, thinking that she cleaned up pretty good for a whore.

She ran down the backstairs into the room where she normally ate breakfast and helped Mr. Vander with the books. He was sitting at the table reading the newspaper. "Mr. Vander, I have to leave. It's an emergency and I can't explain now. I will tell you everything when I get back. Don't say anything to anybody about my leaving," she said.

Mr. Vander lowered his paper and peered at her. "Well, alright Miss Mary, but you be careful. I couldn't stand something happening to you," he said.

"I will be," she said as she headed to the back door.

From the alley, she walked as fast as she could to the sheriff's office. There was a note on the door stating that he would not be back until evening. "Damn it," she cursed aloud. "I bet he went to see Ethan."

Mary looked around, trying to think what she would do next when she saw the doctor's office and headed towards it, bursting through the door.

Doctor Abram was asleep at his desk when Mary rushed in, startling him so badly that he jumped to his feet. "Damn, Mary, what in the hell are you in such an all fire hurry about?" he said, clearly irritated.

"Doc, you have to take me out to Ethan's place. I think the sheriff is there and I need to see him now," Mary said.

"What's the problem, Mary?" Doc asked.

"Doc, please, we have got to go now. I'll tell you everything on the way," she pleaded.

Chapter 25

Gideon and Marcus were sitting out on the porch with Ethan as he smoked his pipe. Tension between the two men had eased somewhat as they managed to make small talk, though Gideon continually caught himself thinking that unless Marcus got lucky last night, and he doubted that he did, he and not Marcus was the last person to sleep with Marcus's wife. There was no regret or remorse in his thoughts. In his mind, a love born long ago trumped a marriage certificate even if it had only been for one night. He then banished Abby from his thoughts and starting thinking about Benjamin. Much to his chagrin, he knew that the kidnappers held all the cards. His only option was to react to the hand they dealt. Foreboding that he could not save Benjamin started sinking in.

Ethan took a draw on his pipe, raised his head and blew the smoke into the air. "That looks like Doc Abram's buggy coming. I wonder why he is in such a hurry," he said.

Gideon looked up, watching the buggy scurrying down the road. "There's somebody with him," he remarked.

Doc trotted the buggy right up to the porch. "Is Sheriff Fuller here? Mary has some news," he said.

Gideon could see the surprise on Mary's face upon seeing him standing on the porch. The moment was awkward and he had a feeling it was going to get more so. "The sheriff deputized me. What's the problem?" he asked.

Doc climbed off the buggy and helped Mary down. "We should go inside. Sarah needs to hear this too," he said.

Sarah and Abby looked up as everybody walked into the cabin, obviously surprised to see Doc and Mary. There was an embarrassing silence and nobody seemed to know what to say. Finally, Sarah spoke. "Doc and Mary, good to see you. What brings you out here?"

Doc looked at Mary and realized that he needed to take the lead with her seeming to be too overwhelmed to speak. Looking around the room, he thought that if a boy's life were not in the balance that this gathering would make a great joke about what happens when a preacher, a whore, and star-crossed lovers enter a room. "Mary has some news about Benjamin. Go ahead and tell them, Mary," he said.

Mary was looking down, playing with her hands. She had never felt more embarrassed about being a whore or how low her life had sunk. If not for Benjamin's sake, she would have run from the house. "Uh, Jasper, Frank DeVille's ranch hand, came into the salon today and I sat down at the table with him. I mentioned the kidnapping and I could just tell that he was lying and knew something about it. Jasper's not the smartest man alive and he can't lie for nothing. So, I, uh, uh, tricked him into telling me everything. Frank is in on it and Hank Sligo kidnapped Benjamin and took him to Moccasin Cave."

"I checked Moccasin Cave. I didn't see anything and I looked for tracks and everything," Marcus interrupted.

"Unless you had a torch to go back in there, you wouldn't have seen them if they were lying low," Gideon said.

Marcus sat down, feeling as if he had let everybody down. It seemed to him that he always failed when he was needed the most. "I'm sorry," he said."

Mary resumed telling her news. "Jasper and Walter, the other ranch hand, have been staying with him there all this time. I guess Jasper couldn't take it any longer and came to town for some whiskey. Sligo is going to the cave in the morning to tell them the plans for tomorrow. Jasper didn't know what the plans were, just his and Walter's escape plan," she said.

"Son of a bitch," Gideon said. "I never thought DeVille would stoop so low."

Ethan rubbed his forehead, feeling nearly too weak to continue to stand. "Mary, I don't know how you tricked him, but -," he said before stopping when he realized what he was saying.

Sarah, feeling more alert than she had all week was determined not to seem judgmental. "Mary, God bless you, I don't care how you got the information, just that you did," she said and arose from the table and embraced Mary. She could not let her go, too overcome with emotion and guilt for having ever passed judgment on the life Mary had chosen.

"Gideon, what do you think we should do?" Ethan asked.

"I say we ride towards the cave and wait for nightfall and then I'll go in and get Benjamin. I think it's our best bet," Gideon said.

Sarah released Mary and turned to Gideon. "Gideon, I don't care about the money and besides now that you know where they are, you can catch them when they leave after they give us Benjamin back. They can all stand trial," she said.

"Sarah, it's all open ground around that cave. There is no way we can be close enough in daylight to stop from happening whatever they have planned. Like I said, I never thought Frank would stoop to this, but now that he has, he is too cautious of a man to leave witnesses. I'm sure the plan is to kill the ranch hands, maybe even Sligo, and I fear they will kill Benjamin also, in case he heard something. Sarah, if we wait, they are in control and I don't think Benjamin leaves the cave alive. If we act now, we are in control. Two ranch hands getting surprised in a cave are no match for me. I swear to you that I will get Benjamin out of there. You have to trust me on this," Gideon said.

"Gideon is right, Sarah. We need to get Benjamin tonight. I'd rather trust Gideon to succeed than Frank to do the right thing," Ethan said.

Sarah could feel the anger rushing over her at the thought that a sad pathetic man more worried about building a cattle empire than his or anybody else's happiness had tried to destroy them over a land deal. "That bastard stole Benjamin because we were going to buy the Holden place. He wanted to ruin us over a piece of land," she said.

The realization of the truth in Sarah's words hit Ethan hard. His own need to become a big time rancher had led to this. "Sarah, I am sorry," Ethan said. "I never would have wanted that land for all the money in the world if had known it would lead to this. I should have been happy with what God has blessed us with."

"Ethan, I will have none of that kind of talk," Sarah said. "It is not a sin for a man to want to better his family by honest means. This is all on Frank DeVille. The rest of us are just his victims. Do not feel guilty again. I won't have it."

Abby wanted to reassure Ethan in hopes that he would realize that nobody blamed him. "Ethan, Sarah is right, you are blameless in this. Nobody should go through life avoiding their dreams for fear of evil," she said.

Ethan did not say anything, but went to where his gun belt hung and grabbed it.

"Hold on a minute," Sarah said. "Isn't there still time to eat and get over to that cave before sunset? There's no need riding over there and waiting for dark with your bellies' growling."

"Sarah is right. We have time and I can always find an excuse for Sarah's cooking," Gideon said, trying to lighten the mood.

Doc decided that is was time for Mary and him to take their leave. He did not think they would want her at their supper table. "Well, Mary and I best be getting back to town," he said.

"Since when did you ever pass up one of my meals? You don't look sickly to me and Mary is going to be our guest of honor. That's the least I can do for the lady. I don't know where we would be without her help," Sarah said.

"Ma'am, that is not necessary. You don't need me sitting at your table, and besides, I should be getting back," Mary said.

"I won't take no for an answer. Anybody that tries to save my child will always be welcome at my table. And don't call me ma'am. I'm Sarah, same as I always was," Sarah said.

"Sarah, may I help you cook the meal? It's been a long time since I helped cook a real meal," Mary said.

"Sure. Me, you, and Abby will get these boys fed in no time," Sarah said.

The women prepared the meal and brought it to the table as everybody gathered around for Ethan to say the blessing. Ethan and Gideon did their best to make it seem as if it were a Thanksgiving dinner, telling jokes and reminiscing, but the weight of what was about to happen weighed too heavily on the group for it to be a success until at last, they gave up and everybody ate in silence.

With the meal finished, Marcus asked, "Do you have a horse that I can use? I would like to go with you."

"Sure, Marcus," Ethan said. "I suspect it is time we get to riding."

Sarah walked over to Gideon and kissed him on the cheek. "That's my baby, Gideon. Don't let anything happen to him," she said.

Chapter 26

Gideon, Ethan, and Marcus talked little as they traveled to the cave. Gideon concentrated on the different scenarios that might play out in rescuing Benjamin and how he would react to them. They rode to within an eighth mile of the cave and stopped where the groundcover disappeared and the land turned flat and barren. Tying their horses up behind the tree line, they watched the sun disappearing from sight, waiting on nightfall before they could proceed.

"I haven't been in that cave since we were in our teens. Do you remember it at all?" Ethan asked as they peered out at the cave through the brush.

"Yeah, there is that first room that sunlight comes in and then it bends hard to the right into that big chamber with the water. I bet they are in that part," Gideon said.

"How are you going to do it?" Ethan asked.

"I'm going to walk in as quietly as possible and they will be surprised whether they hear me or not. They'll think it is Sligo if nothing else. The element of surprise gives you one hell of an advantage," Gideon said.

"What if they don't have any light?" Marcus asked.

"I doubt they're going to be sitting in the pitch black, especially now that they have a bottle to share," Gideon said.

"I still can't believe they were there and I missed it," Marcus said.

"You didn't know that you would be checking a cave that day and needing a torch. Let it go. It's going to be alright now," Gideon said.

They waited until the dark made it impossible to see the cave entrance from where they were hid. Satisfied it was time to go, Gideon pulled out his rifle and handed it to Marcus, who was unarmed. "We'll just walk on up there and you two can wait outside. I will holler before I come back out of the cave. So if somebody comes out without yelling, you know it's not me and waylay them," he said.

Now that the time was at hand, Ethan started feeling nauseous with worry. His stomach was churning and the acid was rising up into his throat. He kept thinking of all the things that could go wrong and the heartbreak that it would bring. "Are you sure about this, Gideon?" Ethan asked.

"It's our best chance. After tonight, it gets tricky and they have the advantage. Even if we stopped Sligo from getting to the cave in the morning, we have no idea what these two would do. They'd get nervous and nervous is unpredictable. Relax Ethan, I'm going to get Benjamin out or die trying," Gideon said.

"Maybe I should go in," Ethan said. "It's not right for you to risk your life for us."

"Ethan, for Christ sake, I'm the only one experienced in these kinds of things and that's what friends do. Benjamin saved my life and now I'm going to go get him. Perfect little circle, don't you think? And besides, you might shoot yourself with the way you aim a pistol," Gideon said.

"I'm not half as bad at shooting a pistol as you make me out to be," Ethan said defensively.

"I know, but you're so perfect in every other way that I have to take what I can get to ride you," Gideon said.

"I'll be sure to tell Sarah what you said. I'm sure she'd have something to say about my perfection," Ethan said, realizing Gideon had taken his mind off worrying.

"Let's go," Gideon said and started walking.

The stars and moon lent enough light that navigating across the expanse was not a problem. The little breeze there had been stilled with the darkness and the temperature fell, leaving a nice cool evening. Nobody spoke now, but walked with purpose towards the destination.

At the mouth of the cave, Gideon drew his pistol and cocked it. Closing his eyes, he took a deep breath and let it out slowly along with any tension. The next couple of minutes would decide his and Benjamin's fate and he said a silent prayer that this time he would be saving a child instead of killing one.

He walked into the cave and saw that it was pitch black save for the little light from their fire that danced on the wall where it made the turn into the next room. He wasn't sure why, but he had expected more light and now headed slowly towards the back, trying to feel each step out to avoid tripping on something unseen. He could hear one of the men bragging in a loud voice that he was going to have himself a kept woman with all his money and the other one was trying to get him to take the horses out to graze. A couple of steps from the turn, he kicked a rock, sending it bouncing noisily on the hard surface.

"Is that you, Boss?" a voice called out.

Gideon took the last two steps quickly, spun to the right and surveyed the room. One man was standing, reaching for his gun, and the other was sitting a few feet from Benjamin. He aimed at the middle of the first man's chest and fired. The roar of the shot was deafening in the cave as the sound reverberated off the walls. The bullet lifted the man off his feet and flung him backwards into the pool of water as Gideon fired at the second man just as he dove behind Benjamin.

The man drew his gun and pointed it at Benjamin as he did his best to hide his large frame behind the boy. "Toss your gun away and let me walk out of here if you don't want the boy hurt," he said.

Gideon wished the fire were burning brighter. The large man was exposed behind Benjamin and he could shoot him without endangering the boy, but a little more light would make the task a lot easier. Benjamin looked more relieved to see him than scared of the situation. "I'm the deputy and I can't let you escape. If you want to live, you need to surrender. I want you to testify against Sligo and DeVille. You'll serve some time in prison and then you can get on with your life, otherwise you die," he said.

"Who said anything about Sligo and DeVille?" he said.

"You must be Walter then. Your buddy Jasper went to town today and ran his mouth. If I kill you, they may get away with plotting this all out. You and Jasper will die and take all the blame," Gideon said.

"That damn idiot. One day away from being rich and he can't keep his mouth shut," Walter said. "Unless you don't care if this boy gets killed, you better throw down your gun and let me walk."

"Walter, there is one hole in your logic there. If you shoot Benjamin, I'm going to blow you into hell," Gideon said.

"But can you live with his death on your -," Walter said as Gideon fired his revolver when he saw the man unknowingly lower his gun away from Benjamin's head as he talked.

The boom of the gun was followed by Walter screaming shrilly. Gideon had hit him in the shoulder, sending him flopping backwards with Benjamin in his arms. He had lost his gun and was writhing around, holding his shoulder as Benjamin tried to climb off the flopping man. Gideon put his foot on the gun, reached down with one hand and yanked Benjamin off Walter.

"Are you okay?" Gideon asked as he draped his hand on Benjamin's shoulder and pressed the boy into his leg.

"I'm fine. I knew you and Pa would come for me," Benjamin said.

"Well, you were right. We need to hurry up here before your pa goes crazy waiting outside," Gideon said as he picked up Walter's gun and stuck it in his belt.

"Walter, get up. We are walking out of here right now," Gideon said.

"You shot me. How am I supposed to walk now," Walter said.

"I shot you in the shoulder, not the leg, and I could have killed you if I had wanted. If you don't get up and walk, I'm going to blow your balls off with my next shot. I don't have time for this. Now get up. I'm taking you to jail. It's your decision whether it's with nuts or without," Gideon said and cocked his gun.

Gideon watched Walter find a way to get to his feet at the sound of the gun click. "Lead the way out of here," Gideon said as he grabbed one of their torches lying on the ground and lit it in the fire.

"We're coming out," Gideon yelled when they neared the mouth of the cave.

Walter walked out first, followed by Gideon, and then Benjamin in the rear. Gideon stepped to the side, allowing father and son to see each other, whereupon Ethan dropped to his knees as Benjamin ran into his arms. "Benjamin, are you okay?" Ethan asked.

"I'm hungry. We didn't eat very good in there, but I'm fine," Benjamin said.

"I bet when you get home your momma will fix you anything that you want," Ethan said.

"I knew you and Mr. Gideon would come for me," Benjamin said.

"Well, there are lots of people we need to thank for this moment. I will tell you about that later. Did they hurt you any?" Ethan asked.

"No, nobody hurt me. I just worried a lot," Benjamin said.

"I love you, son," Ethan told him.

"I love you too, Pa," Benjamin answered.

Ethan continued to embrace Benjamin as he slowly began to take stock of the injured man. He stood and took a couple of steps away from Benjamin before gripping his rifle by the barrel. He swung the butt hard into the injured shoulder of Walter and watched as the man screamed and dropped to his knees. Swinging the gun again, he caught him across the shoulder blades and planted him on his face. He felt no guilt for the pleasure he was taking in the man's pain as he ground his foot into Walter's injured shoulder while the screaming became intolerable.

Gideon grabbed Ethan's arm and jerked him away. "You're scaring Benjamin. That's enough. Do you understand?" he said.

Ethan looked at Benjamin and seeing the fear on his face, the feeling of guilt began for assaulting the man in front of his son, but not for actually doing it. In fact, if not for Gideon, he would have still been torturing the man. His hatred was such that the bloodlust he felt was intoxicating. "I'm sorry, Benjamin. That man almost took you from me and I was angry," he said.

Benjamin nodded his head, trying not to cry at seeing a scary side to his father.

Gideon needed to get things back on track. There was a lot to do and Benjamin needed to get home to Sarah. "Benjamin and Ethan stay here with the prisoner and Marcus and I will go back in the cave to saddle their horses and load up Jasper," he said before leaning into Ethan's face. "Get a hold on yourself, because tomorrow, the preacher in you is not going to be happy with the part that turned vigilante."

Gideon and Marcus emerged from the cave a short time later leading the two horses with Jasper draped over one of them. Walter had regained enough of his composure to fear Ethan and seemed happy to see Gideon return to have his hands tied and helped into the saddle.

Gideon took the reins of both horses and started walking. "When we get back to our horses, you two can get Benjamin back to his momma and I'll take these two into town. Doc can fix Walter up and I'll see if Sligo is in one of the saloons," he said.

"You're not going to go after Sligo by yourself, are you? Wait until morning and me and half the town would probably join you," Ethan said as he walked beside Gideon.

"If he is in town, I am. I've already gotten the better of him twice. He's scared of me," Gideon said.

"Don't get overly confident there. That's a good way to get killed," Ethan said.

"You just need to get on back home. I have not lived this long by being overly confident. Maybe I should start helping you with your sermons," Gideon chided.

They reached their horses and Gideon lifted Benjamin up behind Ethan after he had mounted. "I'll see you two later tonight or in the morning," he said.

"You came back for me. I knew you would," Benjamin said.

"You probably let them kidnap you just to get me back here," Gideon said and patted the boy's leg.

"Gideon, wait for morning so that me and the sheriff and others can help you. Benjamin is safe and the rest can wait," Ethan said.

Gideon did not answer. If he got the chance to end it tonight, he would. The last thing he needed was for Ethan to get killed trying to help.

Marcus handed Gideon back his rifle without either man speaking. Now that their mission was over, they could get back to not liking each other.

Gideon mounted and headed towards town with Jasper and Walter in tow while Ethan, Marcus, and Benjamin headed for home. Ethan rode as fast as the night allowed, knowing that Sarah was sitting on pins and needles waiting for their return. Once they reached the road home, they could see lanterns shining from the porch.

"Looks like you got a welcoming party for you," Ethan said.

Sarah, Abby, and Winnie were all standing anxiously on the porch as they rode into the yard. "Momma, I'm back," Benjamin shouted out before they could see him in the dark.

Sarah could not move. Her feet seemed to be frozen to the porch. She could only rock her body and cover her face with her hands as the reality set in that the ordeal was finally over. Benjamin ran up onto the porch, wrapping his arms around his mother and squeezing. His touch brought her out of her stupor and she squatted down and hugged him back. "Oh, I've missed you. I didn't know what I was going to do if I never got you back," she said before crying too hard to continue.

"It's alright, Momma. They didn't hurt me and I'm going to be more careful from now on so that it doesn't happen again. I promise," Benjamin said.

"Where is Gideon?" Abby asked, hearing the panic in her own voice betray her emotions.

Marcus heard it too. It was at that moment that he knew that he had lost the love of his wife if he had ever had it in the first place. He had always been good to Abby and tried to love her the best that he knew how, but it always seemed that their marriage had lacked the spark of other couples that they knew. Winnie was their only testament to their years of marriage.

"He rode into town with the kidnappers. Jasper is dead and Walter is shot," Ethan said.

Ethan gently helped Sarah to the swing, sitting down beside her and motioning for Benjamin to sit between them. He was worried how much of a toll this had taken on his wife. She had always bounced back from the miscarriages, but he feared this had been worse. "We're all together now. It's time to relax," Ethan said.

Winnie walked over and leaned in, kissing Benjamin on the cheek. "I'm sorry I hit you when you kissed me. I won't do it whenever you want to kiss me again," she said.

The four adults laughed, releasing the tension all of them were feeling for their own different reasons.

Chapter 27

Gideon rode into town, pulling his horse up in front of the doctor's office. The ride had been uneventful except for listening to Walter yap about how sorry he was about being part of the kidnapping until Gideon told him to shut up. A light was on inside, which he found a bit surprising. He guessed Doc Abram was expecting him to bring him some business or Doc thought he would be the business.

"Come on and get down, Walter. Doc Abram can treat your wound," Gideon said.

"I don't think I can walk, like I might collapse. I feel awfully weak," Walter said.

"Well then, you are going to die in the street, because I'm not dragging your ass in," Gideon said as he tied the horses and started walking towards the door.

"Wait, help me down and I'll manage to walk," Walter said.

Gideon helped him off the horse and followed him into the office. Doc Abram and Sheriff Fuller were sitting at the desk with a bottle of bourbon and two glasses half-empty. "I see you were expecting some business. I sure as hell hope that you weren't expecting it to be me," Gideon said.

"No, sir, I did not. Did you get Benjamin?" Doc asked as he motioned for Walter to lie down.

"He should be back home with his momma by now. He seems to have come through it pretty good for a little boy," Gideon said.

"I knew that you'd get him as soon as Mary told me what had happened. I see Jasper was the unlucky one. Kind of poetic justice for the big mouth. I really thought that they would both be dead. That would be preferable treatment for somebody abducting children," Doc said as he started cutting Walter's shirt away.

"I wanted this one alive to implicate Sligo and DeVille," Gideon said.

"I'm sorry I couldn't have been of some assistance, Gideon. By the time I found out about what was going on, I knew that there was no point in trying to get to the cave," Sheriff Fuller said.

"It all worked out just fine. I owed Benjamin anyway," Gideon said.

"Is there anything else that I need to know?" Sheriff Fuller asked.

"No, I don't think so. I guess we should ask Walter here his side of things," Gideon said.

"Walter, I can have a lot of sway with the judge if you give me a reason. Tell me who was behind all of this?" the sheriff said.

Walter was making all kinds of sounds of discomfort as the doctor probed the wound. "Sligo did the kidnapping. DeVille ordered us to watch the boy," he said in stilted language through the pain.

"I never thought Frank DeVille amounted to a horse turd, but I never dreamed he would pull this. We're going to make him pay," Sheriff Fuller said.

"Mary didn't go back to work, did she?" Gideon asked.

"She went back to the saloon. I don't know if she is working or not. I have not made it down there yet," Doc said, annoyed that work had interfered with his plans.

"I think Walter has all the fight out of him, but just in case, do you still have the scatter gun handy that you used to blow Durango Dick to hell?" Gideon asked and watched to see if Walter was listening. The question had gotten his attention.

"I sure do. Don't worry about me," Doc said as he continued working on Walter's shoulder.

"What's the plan, Sheriff?" Gideon asked.

"Sligo was in the Last Chance the last time that I checked and he shouldn't have a clue that we are onto him. We'll just walk in and get close enough to get the drop on him. Shouldn't be any gunfire that way. It has been my experience that the wrong person usually gets shot when a gun goes off in a saloon," the sheriff said as he headed out the door.

Hank Sligo was sitting at the end of the bar near the door that led to the back room. He was flush with nervous energy, ready for tomorrow to be over. Every time a patron came through the door, he checked to see if it was the doctor. Doc Abram usually beat him to the bar and he was anxious to ply him with a beer to get the old gossiper to talk.

The doors swung open as Sheriff Fuller and Gideon walked into the Last Chance. Something did not seem right about it to Sligo. The doctor was already missing from his normal spot and seeing the two lawmen coming into the saloon together did not strike him as a social visit. One thing the war had taught him was to trust his instincts and his instincts told him to run. He smoothly moved through the door into the back.

Mr. Vander looked up from working on his books. "You no belong back here. You get out of here," he said.

Sligo walked past him without acknowledging the old German and out the back door into the alley. The sky was dark enough to provide him some cover to walk away from the downtown. He hoped to circle back for his horse to escape to DeVille's place. His mind was racing trying to figure out how they could know that he was involved or if he was simply being paranoid on the last evening of waiting.

"Sligo, stop. You are under arrest," Gideon shouted breathlessly from the end of the alley.

There was enough light behind Gideon that Sligo could make out his silhouette clearly, whereas he knew that he had to be almost invisible in the darkness. Seeing the barrel of his gun well enough to aim was the problem, but he wasn't going to pass up his best chance at killing the blue-belly. He pointed it at Gideon and fired.

Gideon heard the bullet whiz past his ear and dropped to the ground just as a second shot was fired. He could barely see Sligo running away down the alley, making it pointless to shoot at him. A bullet shot in the dark would be more apt to find the wrong target than it would Sligo.

Gideon ran back to the front of the saloon to find Sheriff Fuller who had retrieved his shotgun. "Sheriff, I'm going to try and find him and put an end to this. If I don't, he will try to get back to his horse and ride to DeVille. Why don't you stand there in the shadows and if he gets on his horse, blow him off it," Gideon said.

"I'll be waiting on him. Be careful, Gideon. That is one mean son of a bitch," the sheriff said.

Gideon started walking down Main Street. The town was unusually quiet with the piano music that normally drifted out of the Last Chance silenced by the commotion. The street lamps provided enough light that he would be able to see Sligo, but also made him and easy target. He headed towards the livery stable figuring that Sligo would either try to steal a horse or circle back for his own mount to get back to DeVille. A block down from the saloon, he heard the sound of wood splintering as a door gave way. Gideon looked in the direction of the noise and caught sight of Sligo entering the dry goods store across the street. He guessed Sligo was going to steal guns or ammo.

Gideon jogged down the street and squatted behind a water trough directly across the street from the store. He cursed himself for not grabbing his rifle as he waited for Sligo to emerge from the store. It sounded as if he was tearing everything apart inside with glass breaking and things crashing. The noise stopped as Sligo walked out of the store carrying a rifle and paused, seeming unsure on which way he wanted to go.

Gideon poked his head and arms above the trough, aiming his revolver at Sligo. "Throw down your guns. It's over, Sligo," he shouted.

Sligo drew his pistol and fired twice. Gideon could hear the thud of the bullets as they struck the water trough. He shot once and Sligo screamed, dropping the rifle as he grabbed his knee before collapsing.

Gideon stood to get a better view. "Throw out your guns," he repeated.

Sligo aimed his revolver and fired two more shots. One of them struck the wooden sign above Gideon's head and splinters of wood fluttered down on him. A fury came over him as he realized that his adversary would not surrender. Sligo represented everything bad that had ever happened in his life and he was going to kill him for it. He started striding towards him, too enraged to worry about his own safety. Sligo seemed determined to get a shot off with the rifle instead of firing at him with the pistol. He used the rifle to get to his feet and then tried to stand on one leg and aim the weapon. Gideon hated Sligo, wanting to torture him and make him suffer. The man had caused enough pain and now he would suffer for it. Instead of aiming for his chest to kill him, he fired three shots into Sligo's enormous stomach, knocking him backwards through the window of the store.

Gideon ran up to the window and looked in. From the light of the street lamp, he could see Sligo lying there moaning and holding his stomach. The rage in him was ready to inflict more pain if given the chance, but Sligo had no fight left in him. "You dumb son of a bitch, you should have surrendered when I gave you the chance. See you in hell," he said.

Gideon reloaded his revolver and walked slowly back down the street. Guilt started creeping into his conscience with each step. He knew that he had no choice but to kill Sligo, but he should have done it mercifully. He had seen enough men in the war die from gut shots to know that an agonizing death awaited Sligo.

He met Sheriff Fuller walking towards him as fast as the old sheriff's legs would carry him. "We need some of the men from the saloon to carry Sligo to Doc. He's in the dry good store, but he won't make it," Gideon said.

"You had me scared there. I thought that maybe he got you. Sure glad it was the other way around and we're all better off with him dead anyway," Sheriff Fuller said. "That just leaves DeVille then."

"I'm going to the saloon to get the men. I'll meet you at Doc's office," Gideon said.

"Okay, but when you get there, if Doc is finished with Walter, I want you to take him and lock him in the jail. I'm going to try to get Sligo to name DeVille in all this. I figure he might be more apt to talk if you aren't around and that'll give us another person implicating him at trial," the sheriff said.

A crowd, including Mary, was waiting outside the saloon when Gideon walked up. They were standing quietly watching him. Mary looked as if the day's events had exhausted her and he could see the stress around her mouth and eyes. She was still wearing the clothes that she had on at the cabin and she looked out of place amongst the saloon patrons. "Benjamin's at home. He is going to be fine," he called out to her.

She smiled meekly at him and mouthed, "Thank you."

"I need some of you men to help me carry Sligo to Doc Abram's office. He's in no shape to walk," Gideon said.

Gideon and the other men labored to carry Sligo towards the doctor office. It seemed as if they were on the verge of dropping him every step of the way. His shirt and pant leg were covered in blood and he reeked of sweat and feces. Moaning and screaming every step of the way, by the time they lifted Sligo up onto the table, he was cussing them all out and threatening their lives.

Doc Abram looked at the three bullet holes in the shirt taut over Sligo's protruding belly and then looked over at Gideon. "Looks like you made sure you got him," he said.

Sheriff Fuller looked over at Walter sitting over in a corner with his arm in a sling. "Are you finished with Walter?" he asked.

"He's good to go. I will come over to the jail tomorrow and check on him," Doc said.

After the room cleared of the volunteers and Gideon had led out Walter, Sligo calmed down while the doctor started cutting off his clothes. Sheriff Fuller walked over to him. "Hank, this is Sheriff Fuller. Jasper is dead and Walter is in jail. I need for you to tell me who else is involved with the kidnapping," he said.

Sligo looked up at him, his eyes were glazed over, and he squinted to make them focus. Laboring for breath, he had to inhale deeply before speaking. "This was all DeVille's idea. I knew it was a bad one. Should have never gone along with it," he said and closed his eyes.

"Hank, DeVille is going down too," Sheriff Fuller said.

"How did you figure it out?" Sligo managed to ask.

"Jasper came to town for whiskey and talked a little too much," the sheriff said.

"I told Frank that we should give them a bottle. I'm going to die over a bottle of whiskey," Sligo whispered.

The sheriff stepped outside where Gideon was waiting. Sheriff Fuller said, "Let's get DeVille in the morning. I think we've had enough excitement for one day. I'll meet you at dawn at the road that leads to DeVille's house. You go get you some rest, you hear?"

Chapter 28

On the way back home from the Oakes' cabin, the conversation between Marcus and Abby never strayed from Benjamin and the kidnapping. Both of them seemed as if they were afraid to broach any other subject for fear of where it might lead and they masked the tension between them with politeness.

Marcus waited until they were home and Winnie was asleep before approaching Abby. "If you ever did love me, you don't anymore do you?" he asked.

Abby looked up at him in surprise. A direct question from Marcus about how she felt was the last thing that she was expecting. Talking about ones feelings was not something he ever did. "What are you talking about?" she asked, feigning ignorance.

"Abby, I heard the sound of your voice when you thought something had happened to Gideon. It wasn't sadness. It was a panic as if you saw your future slipping right away from you," Marcus said.

She realized that she could not play the game of pretending a minute longer. The facade was dragging her down like a weight and she was ready to unburden herself from it. "Okay, Marcus, I never stopped loving Gideon, it's true. And him coming back has opened up a lot of feelings that have been buried a very long time. I thought I was over it, but I was wrong," she said.

"Do you love me?" Marcus asked as he dropped into a chair.

"Marcus, we have a good marriage in its own way. We get along fine, you are good to me, and you gave me Winnie. I can't imagine my life without her. But no, I don't love you. When we got married, I thought I did, but I came to realize that there is a difference between being lonely and being in love. I know this must hurt you and I am sorry for that, but you asked and I don't want to pretend any longer. I wasn't ready for this conversation. In fact, I don't know that I ever would have been, but now we're having it," Abby said.

Marcus could feel his face flush and he thought he might get sick to his stomach. Abby was the only women he had ever loved and now he knew that her feelings for him were no more real than the elixirs that the traveling medicine men sold to their gullible customers. He wanted to break something, but he was much too self-controlled ever to do that. Finally, marshaling the courage, he asked, "Do you want a divorce?"

Abby sat down at the table across from him. She wished that he had been content to enjoy the blessing of having Benjamin returned safely and left it at that. "I don't know. We have a life together that I am not sure that I am ready to throw away and there's Winnie to think about. There's also the scandal that it would cause. Our marriage is never going to be what I want it to be, but it is something," she said.

Marcus looked her in the eyes and cleared his throat. "There's something that I think I figured out last summer that I didn't really want to know the answer to, but now I do. You and Joann were walking out in the orchard and you looked so much alike that I thought that you could really tell that your mothers were sisters and then it occurred to me that you favor your father's side of the family. I put it all together then, her blue eyes, that you went to Wyoming that summer to have a baby, and the name Joann is for Johann. Joann is your and Gideon's daughter, isn't she?" Marcus said.

Abby's heart was pounding so hard that she could feel her temples moving in and out. She had always been surprised that no one had ever figured it out and now it had finally happened. "Yes," she said quietly.

Marcus's stomach started to churn violently. "Quite a secret to take to our wedding bed," he said.

"Yes, Marcus, it was," Abby said.

"Does he know?" he asked.

"He just found out on the way back from me tracking him down," she said.

Marcus jumped up and ran out the front door. She could hear him retching off the porch. As much as she wanted to feel bad about all of the things that she had told him, relief that all the secrets were exposed is what came over her. She did not have to pretend any longer.

Chapter 29

Gideon awoke to the smell of coffee. It was still dark out with the only light coming from an oil lamp by the cook stove. It took him a moment to realize that he was lying on a pallet in front of Ethan's fireplace. Yesterday's events had left him sore and his limbs seemed so heavy that he wondered if he could drag them over to the table. He had slept hard with the satisfaction of knowing that Benjamin was safe in his room, but his mind and body had been through too much in the last few days to recover with one good night of sleep. Sitting up, he saw Ethan cracking eggs. "You're up early," he said.

"I'm going with you this morning," Ethan said.

"Ethan, that's not necessary. Sheriff Fuller and I can take care of it. You have been through enough and the last thing Sarah needs is for something to happen to you now. Just let me handle it," Gideon said.

"Gideon, I'm either going to watch that son of a bitch die or he is going to have to look me in the eye when he surrenders," Ethan said.

In the old days, Gideon had usually been able to talk Ethan into coming around to his point of view, but looking at Ethan's determined posture, he knew there was no chance on this day. "I guess you deserve the satisfaction of that. Let's have some of your coffee and eggs then. I sure hope the food don't kill me before I get DeVille," Gideon said with a wink.

∞

The sun was starting to pinken the sky in the east when they rode up to Sheriff Fuller waiting for them near Frank DeVille's ranch. "I see you brought reinforcements," he said.

"He wouldn't listen. I tried to get him to stay," Gideon said.

"Let's go get him," the sheriff said as he turned his horse and headed toward DeVille's house.

DeVille had had a fitful night of sleep. He was so wound up worrying about everything going right with the picking up of the ransom and Sligo killing everybody at the cave that he could barely close his eyes. Several times he had almost walked to the bunkhouse to find out if Sligo had learned anything in town, but each time he convinced himself that if there had been any news, Sligo would have busted down his door knocking.

Just before dawn, he got up and dressed. He was too nervous to eat and instead drank a glass of scotch to calm himself. With the drink finished, he walked into the bunkhouse, struck a match, and lit the lamp on the table. The two new ranch hands were asleep in their bunks, but there was no sign of Sligo. In fact, he could see no sign that Sligo had ever returned from town.

He tried to remember the new men's names, but was at a complete loss as to what they were. "Hey, you two," he called out. "Where is Sligo?"

One of the men roused from his sleep, looking around groggily before focusing on DeVille. "He wasn't back by the time we turned in. I guess he never made it back," he said.

DeVille started to feel weak and wanted to sit. Sligo might annoy the hell out of him, but he was way too dependable not to have returned without something having gone astray. His mind raced on what could have gone wrong and what next to do. He couldn't just run off and leave everything he had spent his life building. His only option he decided was to go to town and see what had happened to Sligo, and if Sligo or the other two had implicated him, he would get the best lawyer in Denver for his defense.

He saddled up and started the ride to town. As the sun's first rays lit the land, he saw the three riders coming his way. He could not recognize them, but knew it had to be Sheriff Fuller, Gideon, and someone else. Knowing that somehow he had been found out, he realized that they were coming to lock him up like a common criminal. The thought made him claustrophobic and he was having trouble breathing as if he were suffocating. He needed to run and he turned his horse around, putting his spurs to it.

Ethan spotted DeVille first, pointing him out to the other two. "He spotted us and is running," he said just as DeVille took off.

"I wonder where the fool thinks he is going," Sheriff Fuller said. "Boys, you're going to have to go get him. I can't ride that hard anymore. Be careful."

Without speaking, Gideon and Ethan both put their horses into a lope, content to keep DeVille in sight until his galloping horse wore down. After a few minutes, they could see DeVille's horse start to slow and he was no longer gaining ground on them.

"He's headed towards the mountains. Must be going to take cover and make a stand," Gideon hollered to Ethan.

"I hope we catch him before he does," Ethan hollered back.

DeVille looked over his shoulder, cursing himself for running his horse so hard. The riders were now gaining rapidly on him. There was no cover for another half mile where the mountain started. He kicked the horse hard in the ribs and it took off in a gallop again, but was so winded that it started slowing back down almost immediately.

Ethan and Gideon put their horses into a gallop, closing distant between them and DeVille quickly. Ethan's mustang, Pie, was a faster horse than Gideon's Buck and he started to pull away. DeVille pulled out his revolver and shot as Ethan closed to within fifty yards. The bullet missed, but Ethan moved Pie directly behind Deville so that he would have to turn sideways to fire another shot. It was the first time that he had ever been fired upon and it seemed as if his heart started racing as fast as the pounding hoof beats. He started to reach for his rifle, but hesitated. As much as he hated DeVille for what he had done, he could not bring himself to shoot him. He grabbed his rope and made a lasso as DeVille fired again. Pie flinched, almost causing Ethan to lose his balance, and for a moment he thought that the horse was shot, but it kept on running. He was directly behind DeVille now and he said a prayer that all his years of roping would pay off as he let the rope sail before another shot could be fired. The rope settled over DeVille as Ethan pulled his horse up hard. DeVille flew off the back of his horse, landing hard on his back and bouncing a foot into the air.

Ethan jumped down ready to pound Frank into submission, but DeVille did not attempt to arise. As Ethan neared him, he could see blood coming from Frank's ears and mouth while his body trembled all over. He walked in front of DeVille and they made eye contact just as Gideon ran up to them. "Why did you do this, Frank? You had everything. What more could you have wanted?" Ethan asked.

DeVille spit out blood. "You win," he said, closing his eyes and going still.

Gideon reached down and touched his neck, feeling for a pulse. "He's dead," he said quietly.

Ethan kicked at the dirt and walked around in a circle. "I hated the son of a bitch and wished him dead, but I didn't want to be the one to do it," he said.

"You tried to take him in. I would have shot him anyway, if you hadn't been in my way. No need to blame yourself, Ethan. It's poetic justice, I believe," Gideon said.

Chapter 30

Gideon and Ethan rested the horses thirty minutes before hoisting DeVille, with considerable effort, across the back of his horse. It took both of the men to stand the large body up beside the horse and as Ethan held him, Gideon ran to the other side and pulled as Ethan lifted to get him across the saddle.

"That was more work than catching him," Gideon said.

"I hope I'm never part of any of this again," Ethan said. He was still trying to come to terms with having been the cause of DeVille's death and touching the body forced him to fight off gagging.

"I know. Let's get back to the sheriff. I imagine he wonders what's going on," Gideon said.

They found the sheriff napping under a tree near where they had left him. He roused from sleep at the sound of the horses. "You had to kill him, I see," Sheriff Fuller said matter-of-factly.

"I see that you were beside yourself with worry about our wellbeing," Gideon said.

"I knew Frank was no match for you two. He never was and I knew he wouldn't be now," the sheriff said.

"He did all the shooting. Ethan roped him, but the fall killed him anyway," Gideon said.

"Serves him right. He and his daddy were a lot alike and they died the same way. Kind of ironic. Let's get back to town," Sheriff Fuller said.

As they rode into Last Stand, the people on the streets stopped and whispered at seeing Frank DeVille's ignoble body hanging over a horse. Most of them had had some dealings with him and few had come away happy about it. Some of the people followed them down the street where the sheriff left the body with the cabinetmaker that doubled as an undertaker.

"I want to go see Doc to check Sligo's condition," the sheriff said as they hitched the horses in front of the jail.

The smell and sound of Hank moaning hit the three men when they walked into the doctor's office. Ethan had to will himself not to throw up on the spot. He had smelled some bad things in his life, but nothing compared to the smell coming out of Sligo.

"Good morning, gentlemen," Doc Abram said.

"Good God, Doc, what is that smell and how do you stand it?" Sheriff Fuller asked.

"That is the smell of intestines leaking everywhere. Pleasant isn't it?" Doc said and looked at Gideon.

"Do you have something that you want to say to me?" Gideon asked tersely.

"You should have killed him instead of this. You are better than that, Gideon," the doctor said.

Gideon first instinct was to defend himself and make his case, but he knew the doctor was right. "I know," was all that he said.

"What happened with DeVille?" the doctor asked.

"He died falling off his horse when we were chasing him. I think it fractured his skull," Sheriff Fuller said.

"It's hard to imagine owning all that DeVille did and coming up with a foolish plan like this. Greed makes a man blind, I guess," Doc said.

Ethan nodded at Sligo. "What about him?" he asked.

"He's delirious now and I doubt he'll come out of it again. The one good thing about not killing him on the spot was that before he got bad, I questioned him some more. He knew he was dying and I think he wanted to clear his conscience. Mary saved Benjamin's life. The plan was for Sligo to kill Walter, Jasper, and Benjamin this morning. He also confessed to killing Mary's husband Eugene," Doc said.

Between the smell and the thought of how close he had come to losing his son, Ethan had to get out of the office. He rushed outside, sitting down on a bench. Unable to hold his emotions in check any longer, he started to cry. The sobs racked his body and he looked around to see if anybody was watching him. He wasn't even sure why he was crying, but he could not stop. The ordeal had finally caught up with him and now that it was over, it all had hit him right between the eyes.

Gideon walked out and sat down beside him. He didn't say anything, just took off his hat and ran his fingers along the brim.

"I'm sorry," Ethan managed to say.

"You don't have anything to apologize about to me. If I had just been through what you have, I would be crying to. I just learned how to do it again myself. Kind of cleans out the poison, I think," Gideon said.

Ethan wiped his nose on the back of his hand and chuckled. "Gideon Johann crying. Now that would be something. Gideon, do you ever think how crazy life can be? A little boy is out exploring against his mother's wishes and finds a man half-dead and that man turns out to be his father's best friend that has been missing eighteen years and then weeks later that man saves that little boy's life. Like you said, a perfect little circle. And Mary – this community never did her right, including me. We all turned our backs on her when Eugene was killed. They weren't from here and didn't matter. I knew what we did was wrong and I didn't do enough to make a difference. A preacher should be the conscience of the community. If anybody should have cared less about what happened to anybody around here, it would have been

Mary and yet she did God knows what to save Benjamin's life. It is all so overwhelming," he said.

"Mary saved Benjamin. I just retrieved him. You could have done it same as me," Gideon said.

"I doubt that. I would have hesitated and lost the advantage," Ethan said.

"I don't think when it comes to Benjamin that you would have hesitated. You would have been just fine," he said.

"All the same, I'm glad I had you to take care of it," Ethan said.

Gideon leaned back, stretching out his legs and crossing them while resting his hands on his stomach. He blew out a breath of air, puffing up his cheek as the air escaped. "That day I cleaned my mother's gravesite, I was finally able for the first time to say out loud what I had done and then I was able to tell Abby and my confession was such a relief to finally share. And now you are the other person that deserves to know," he said and looked around to make sure that no one was in listening distance. "I killed a boy about Benjamin's age running through the brush when I thought we were being attacked. I've been running from it ever since then. It has haunted me and chased me all over the west."

Ethan didn't say anything as he thought about what Gideon had been going through all of those years. His mind went over it slowly and methodically until he felt he fully grasped it. "Gideon, I'm sorry that you had to endure that. It must have been a terrible burden to carry and I wish that you had come back here sooner. Maybe we could have helped you years ago," he said.

"It doesn't matter now and I don't think it would have helped anyway. I think now was the right time to come back. Kind of like fate, maybe," Gideon said.

"So have you put the past behind you and are you ready to start a new life?" Ethan asked.

Gideon uncrossed his legs and crossed them back again with the opposite leg. "I don't know yet. The last few days have been such a whirlwind that I don't know if it is still chasing me or not. Just hard to say," he said.

"I hope and believe it has released you. Like you said, I think fate had to play into this. While it will never bring that little boy back, saving Benjamin had to be redemption for it. I believe it has to be God's plan. It is time to forgive yourself and make a life," Ethan said.

Sheriff Fuller walked out of the doctor's office and slowly inhaled a big breath of air. "That'll ruin your appetite for a while. You boys might as well go on home. This is over with until Walter's trial and I'll let you know when the judge gets to town," he said.

Gideon stood up and pulled off his badge, handing it to the sheriff. "Won't be needing this anymore," he said.

"Thank you for all that you did. I don't know what I would have done without you. I'm too old for this job and I know it. If you decide to stay around, I would be willing to retire and let you take the job. It's time for a younger man," the sheriff said.

"I don't know what I'm going to be doing next, but I appreciate the offer. I'll keep it in mind," Gideon said.

"Let's go home. Maybe I can talk Sarah into cooking us a late breakfast where the eggs aren't so chewy," Ethan said.

Sheriff Fuller placed his hand on Ethan's arm as he started to walk towards his horse. "Don't beat yourself up about what happened out there. You tried to bring him in and it just didn't work. I think we should just say that he fell off his horse. It isn't a lie and that's all anybody needs to know," he said.

Ethan nodded his head solemnly and mounted his horse. "We'll be seeing you, Sheriff," he said.

The day was warming, getting near noontime, as they headed out of town. The horses kicked up puffs of dust as they trotted at a leisurely pace down the road towards home. They had ridden a few minutes when Gideon pulled Buck to a walk. "Slow down," he hollered at Ethan.

"What's the matter?" Ethan asked.

"I wasn't finished with our conversation when the sheriff interrupted us," Gideon said.

"What is it?" Ethan said as he fell in beside Gideon.

"Did you ever meet Abby's niece, Joann?" Gideon asked.

"Sure. She came to church every Sunday with them when she visited for the summers. She also came over with Abby and Winnie to visit Sarah a few times. Sweet girl," Ethan said.

"I just found out about her when Abby tracked me down for Benjamin. This feels so strange to say, but she is really mine and Abby's daughter," Gideon said.

"Oh, my God," Ethan said as he formed a mental picture of the girl, going over her every feature.

"I know," Gideon said. "It's something that I never imagined. As if there hasn't been enough going on, I learn that I am a father."

"Now that I know, I can see the resemblance. She has your crazy blue eyes. What do you think about it all?" Ethan said.

"I don't know. I would like to see her if she felt the same way. She knows the truth about all of it," Gideon said.

"You still love Abby, don't you?" Ethan asked.

"You know, Ethan, that first day that she came into Benjamin's room, I didn't even recognize her, but that voice echoed through me and made me feel things that I didn't know were still alive in me. I guess that's a long way around saying yes. I wish she would have written me during the war and told me that she was carrying our baby. It would have changed our lives. Of course, I could have come home after the war too," Gideon said before falling silent.

They continued riding along at a walk. Ethan was trying to get used to the idea that Abby and Gideon had a daughter together and wondered if it were possible for there to be any more surprises still left to unfold. "So what's next?" he asked.

"I don't have a clue, Ethan. I don't have a clue," Gideon said.

"What do you think that I should do to help Mary out of the life that she lives?" Ethan asked.

"Short of getting me, or some other cowboy to marry her, there is nothing that you can do. It's too late for that," Gideon said.

"Why do you say that?" Ethan asked.

"Well, she can't go work in a store now. No woman in these parts would set foot in it and they sure as hell wouldn't let their husband go in," Gideon said.

"But I got to do something for her," Ethan said.

"Ethan, it's too late. You are right that you and everybody else should have done something a long time ago, but that time has passed. Mary is to blame too. She made her choice. Did you know that she is so good with math that she helps that old German that runs the place do his books? I don't know why she didn't try to get a job as a clerk with somebody," Gideon said.

They rode on in silence for a minute while Ethan mulled over things. "I take it that you know Mary pretty well then?" he asked.

Gideon made a sad smile. "Yes, Ethan, I know her pretty well. She's a good girl, profession aside and a smart one too. She'll find her a man that takes her out of that job one of these days. I just don't think it's me," he said as he put Buck into a trot. "Let's get back, I'm hungry."

Gideon and Ethan found Benjamin out in the yard playing fetch with Chase when they rode into the yard. He looked like a different boy than the one they had brought home the night before, freshly scrubbed and in clean clothes.

"He doesn't look none the worse for wear," Gideon said to Ethan.

"How are you feeling today, son?" Ethan asked.

"I feel good as new," Benjamin said as he ran to them. "Except Momma about scrubbed the hide off me. She wouldn't let me bathe myself. She said I smelled like a turd."

The men burst out laughing. "Well, we couldn't have that now, could we?" Ethan said.

"She keeps coming outside and checking on me and every time she has to hug and kiss on me. It's kind of embarrassing," Benjamin said.

"I bet a warm hug beats sleeping in a cold cave any day of the week though," Gideon said.

"Yes, sir, Mr. Gideon, it does do that," Benjamin said.

Sarah walked out onto the porch. A good night of rest had done much to restore her. The darkness under her eyes was gone and her step had regained its perkiness. A slight paleness was the only remaining sign of the stress that she had lived with for the last week. She was wearing her favorite blue dress and her hair was down on her shoulders, giving her the appearance of a girl much younger than her age.

"Well, look at you," Ethan said. "You look as pretty as the day I met you. I might have to send Gideon and Benjamin off on a horse ride for a while."

"Ethan Oakes, you are incorrigible, talking like that in front of friends and children," Sarah said.

Chapter 31

Sunday afternoon found Gideon and Ethan sitting out on the porch, lazily puffing pipes, blowing great plumes of smoke like Indians sending smoke signals. They had both stuffed themselves on Sarah's fried chicken, mashed potatoes, and gravy. Earlier that day, Gideon had for the first time, gone with the family to hear Ethan preach. He hadn't set foot in a church since the Sunday before he left for the war. He had noticed that Abby seemed uncomfortable with him there and he could feel Marcus staring at him, catching his glares every time he looked towards him.

Ethan took a draw on his pipe, lifted his head and blew the smoke up into the air. "Do you think you might be interested in taking the sheriff's job?" he asked.

"Ethan, I don't know. I feel good right now, but I still don't know how I'm going to feel now that things are starting to calm down. I don't know that I am even capable of changing," Gideon said.

"You've already changed. I can see it. That darkness that you carried when you first got here is gone now. Let it go. It's not a sin to be happy," Ethan said.

Gideon did not respond, leaving the comment hanging before deciding to change the subject. "Are you still going to buy Mr. Holden's place?" he asked.

"I'm going to go see him in the morning and if he still wants to sell it, I'm going back to the bank and see if the loan is still good," Ethan answered.

"I expect all of DeVille's property will go up for sale when the estate gets settled. You could become a land baron," Gideon said.

"I could also have a wife divorce me if I'm not careful. What about you? You could buy the family homestead back and ranch on the side," Ethan said.

"I don't think that a horse and two guns would be enough collateral to use to buy land," Gideon said.

"I think they would loan you the money if you were the sheriff," Ethan said.

Gideon knocked the ash out of the pipe against the heel of his boot. "Somebody is coming," he said and nodded in the direction of the rider. "Looks like Abby."

"That woman is going to ruin my preaching career with all her clandestine meetings with you under my nose," Ethan said half in jest.

"I don't know. She did not act too thrilled to see me at church this morning and I thought Marcus was going to stare a hole through my head," Gideon said as he and Ethan got to their feet to watch her ride in.

Abby had put her horse into a fast lope just before coming into view of the cabin. She knew that she was showing off, but she didn't care. The day was beautiful and she wanted to feel free of the burdens of life and like a girl again. She was wearing the same riding britches that she had worn to find Gideon and a fitted white blouse. Marcus's opinion on such matters did not concern her anymore.

"Good to see you again, Abby," Ethan said as she pulled the horse up in front of the porch. "I hope you didn't lead any Indians to us."

Abby grinned at him. "No. No. Just felt like running a little," she said.

"What do we owe this pleasure?" Ethan asked.

"I'd like to borrow Mr. Johann for a ride. I need to talk to him and then decide if I want to shoot him for all the grief that he has caused me or what," Abby said.

"I expect that you will choose the 'or what' part of it," Ethan said.

Gideon watched the proceedings in amusement. The two were carrying on as if he were not present. He guessed they really didn't care what he thought. Abby was obviously much more relaxed now than she had been at church with Marcus by her side. "Do I get a say in this?" he asked.

Ethan said, "I think your best bet would be to go ride with her and not dally."

Gideon tipped his hat at Ethan. "Yes, sir," he said as he stepped off the porch and headed towards the barn. "You know that all three of us are probably going to hell for this."

When he came out of the barn, it appeared that Ethan, Abby, and now Sarah were still having an animated conversation. He found it odd that Ethan and Sarah were active participants almost to the point of encouragement of something that they would condemn if it were anybody but him and Abby. He rode up to them and said, "Where are we headed?"

"Let's ride to our old picnic spot. I haven't been there since our last picnic," Abby said.

The place Abby was referring to was an aspen grove on a hill tucked away in the corner of Gideon's family homestead. The ride would take a good half hour to reach the spot and they put the horses into a trot, following the creek where Benjamin had found Gideon. They passed the spot where a few weeks earlier Gideon had laid waiting for death and then cut northwest through a valley of wildflowers colored in purple, yellow, and white. Neither of them spoke as they rode, content to be in each other's company one more time. They then crossed the stream where Ethan and Gideon, as teenagers, had spent many an hour fishing and discussing the mysteries of women.

Turning due north, they crossed into the old homestead and soon reached the picnic spot.

Abby jumped from her horse, not bothering to tie it, and ran for an old aspen tree. "Do you think our initials are still there?" she hollered over her shoulder.

Gideon got off his horse and picked up the reins of her mount, tying them both to saplings. "I don't know. I doubt it," he said.

"They're still here," she said, pointing to a weathered spot on the tree where he had planed the bark off with his knife and carved their initials. "It seems like a million years ago when my name was Schone."

"It definitely was a lifetime ago and we thought we had it all figured out back then," he said.

"Just think, Gideon, we made a baby on this very spot," Abby said.

Gideon took her by the arm and turned her towards him. "What are we doing here, Abby? What is this all about?" he asked.

"Come sit with me on our rock. We need to talk," she said.

He followed her as she climbed an outcrop of rocks and sat down on its smooth top. She sat there silently staring at the mountain range miles away, building up her nerve to talk. "The night that you rescued Benjamin, when they came back without you, I panicked and showed a little too much emotion when I asked about you. When we got back home that night, Marcus confronted me about our marriage and you. I couldn't pretend anymore, so I told him how I really felt. I also found out that last summer he had figured out that Joann was ours. I didn't deny that either. He might not have a personality, but the man is intelligent. Marcus knows about everything but what happened on our night on the trail together," she said.

Gideon did not know what to say. A part of him was overjoyed that Marcus knew how she felt and a part of him felt guilty and ashamed to have feelings for another man's wife. He rubbed the back of his neck as he thought about it. "How did he take it?" he finally asked.

"He got sick to his stomach. I feel badly for him. I truly do, but I just couldn't pretend anymore," she said.

Gideon took off his hat and started playing with it. "I told Ethan about Joann. That news was too big to keep bottled up and I had to share it with someone. I've spent a lifetime holding things in and I just don't have it in me to do that anymore," he said.

"I'm glad that you told him. He's good for you. While we were waiting for you to saddle up, he told me that the sheriff offered you his job. Do you think that you will take it?" Abby said.

He let out a sigh, tired of the question. Everybody seemed so certain that he was ready to move on with his life and he wasn't so sure. He had a hard time getting his head around the idea that the past had set him free and was willing to let him settle down. Even though he was ready for a new life and to let the past go, he still feared that it all would come running back with a vengeance. "I don't know. A few good days does not mean that things have changed. I need some time to figure out things," he said.

"If you still want to meet Joann and think that you will be staying around for a while, I will write her and let her know that you are here and see if she wants to come. I think that she will as much as she has asked about you. I'm sure it will catch her by surprise," she said.

Gideon shifted his weight on the rock. All of the questioning was making him uncomfortable. He knew for sure that he wanted to see Joann, but the committing to actually putting it in motion was almost paralyzing. His heart was racing just thinking about it. "I think I can do it, but make sure she only does it because that's what she wants. I don't want to force anything until she is ready. I still haven't quite gotten used to the idea of a daughter and it may take her a while to get used to the idea of meeting me," he said.

Abby patted his leg and smiled at him. "You have my word that I will not push things. It's not what I want to do either and it has to be her choice," she said.

She studied his face. His forehead and eyes betrayed tension and he seemed to be leery of what she might next ask. She patted his leg again. "Gideon, relax. I'm not going to ask you any more questions or expect anything from you. I meant for today to be fun and I can see that you feel like I have put you on the spot. That wasn't my intention. Let's walk a little," she said.

Climbing off the rocks, she took his hand as they walked down the hill to where the land flattened and a small stream cut across the property. Gideon started laughing as they stood watching the water. "Remember that time that you got jealous over that girl that you thought I had eyes for? Sally Jenkins, I think it was, and I talked until I was blue in the face trying to convince you that it was your imagination. I finally got fed up and threw you in the stream and told you that maybe the cold water would bring you to your senses," he said.

Abby laughed at the memory. "I sure do. If you had been wearing a gun that day I would have taken it and shot you for sure," she said.

"Abby, I'm sorry for all the mistakes I made," Gideon said.

She looked up at him and saw that the tension had been replaced by sad regret. He looked like a child on the verge of tears. "We both made a couple of huge mistakes and we both suffered enough for them that apologizing is not necessary and we can't change any of it now anyway. Today and tomorrow is all that matter. I've reached some decisions about my life that I want to share with you and I'm not looking for any answers from you about it. I've decided to divorce Marcus. The one thing that I've realized from your return is that there is a lot more to life than settling for living life being numb. Life should have passion in it and I want that. I feel sorry for Marcus. He deserves better, but I can't live that way any longer. Winnie will have her world turned upside down, but she is strong and will get through it. So, if there ever comes a time in your life where you are ready to settle down, I will be here waiting for you, and if you decide that it will never be possible, you can let me know and I will get on with my life. I will support you in whatever you want to do, if you want to be sheriff, or if you want to ranch, I will use my settlement to help you buy some land. I would love to live here on this place and rebuild the Johann homestead. I have so many wonderful memories of this place. We're still young enough that we could make another baby if we wanted," she said and laughed at the idea.

Gideon took her by both hands and looked her in the eyes. "I hope we get there, Abby. God knows, I hope we get there," he said and kissed her on the lips.

About the Author

Duane Boehm is a musician, songwriter, and author. He lives on a mini-farm with his wife and an assortment of dogs. Having written short stories throughout his lifetime, he shared them with friends and with their encouragement, he has written his second novel *Last Stand*. Please feel free to email him at boehmduane@gmail.com or like his Facebook Page www.facebook.com/DuaneBoehmAuthor.

Made in the USA
Middletown, DE
02 June 2017